(

Elizabeth B. Rennie, the compiler of this book, was a local school teacher who developed an interest in Field Archaeology. She was one of the first students to gain a Certificate in Field Archaeology in the extra-mural course run by Glasgow University. This interest has grown throughout the years and she has now become one of the leading amateur archaeologists in the West of Scotland. She is a founder member of the Cowal Archaeological and Historical Society and her work on what are known as Platform Sites is nationally recognised. She was the first to realise that these sites, of which there are many hundreds in the West of Scotland, are not simply charcoal burning stances as was thought for years but, as a result of her excavations, are habitation sites dating from the 3rd to the 13th century A.D. and earlier.

Cowal

A Historial Guide

Elizabeth B. Rennie

Birlinn

© E. B. Rennie 1993

Published by Birlinn Ltd
13 Roseneath Street
Edinburgh EH9 1JH

Typeset in Monotype Plantin Light by
Koinonia Ltd, Bury
and printed and bound by
Cox and Wyman Ltd, Reading

ISBN 1 874744 08 4

British Library cataloguing-in-publication data
A catalogue record for this book is available
from the British Library

CONTENTS

FOREWORD

The archaeological and historical monuments of Cowal deserve to be better known than they are, particularly as so many remain within settings of great scenic beauty, with views that themselves evoke past times. Today's visitors travel by road along the shores and down the valleys and look out across the lochs and firths little realizing that seaborne travel is the key to understanding the distribution of monuments and the seats of power. The earliest overview of the monuments of Cowal was undertaken by the Ordnance Survey in 1860s in the course of the preparation for the first large-scale maps of Scotland and the notes on antiquities recorded in the Name Books remain an important source of information, particularly about sites that have since been destroyed. Only with systematic field-survey, however, could the full range of antiquities be recorded, and the dedication of the Cowal Archaeological Society in building up a full database of sites cannot be overstated. The country has been explored in a systematic way and all sites have been described, mapped and logged into a Gazetteer – creating one of the first local sites and monuments records in Scotland. The results of several excavations, designed to examine particular problems, have enlarged our knowledge of the dating of other, as yet unexcavated, sites and have extended the date range of other classes of monument.

The Society's decision to present such information in a form that is both comprehensive and comprehensible has been a daunting task and it has been a project that underlies the Society's commitment to the preservation of the archaeology of Cowal. The deep knowledge of the landscape and history of Cowal that Betty Rennie shows in this personal account of the monuments of the peninsula results from many years of indefatigable exploration and recording along with other members of the Society.

In recent years the Royal Commission on the Ancient and Historical Monuments of Scotland was allowed full access to this information in the course of the survey of prehistoric and historic monuments of the peninsula, work that was made more effective and pleasurable through collaboration with the Cowal Archaeological and Historical Society.

The results of archaeological and historical research must continually be made available in a variety of forms to as wide an audience as possible, and the present volume will undoubtedly introduce many readers to a range of monuments in Cowal that forms a microcosm of the archaeology and history of Scotland.

Dr J. N. Graham Ritchie

ACKNOWLEDGEMENTS

This book is greatly accountable to the encouragement and drive of Mr Hubert Andrew. He considered that it must not finish in prehistoric times as its prototype had, but must be taken into the twentieth century and therefore to Mr Andrew most of the chapters about the Medieval and Recent Periods are due. His also are the photographs which represent many hours of tramping over wet hills. I am greatly indebted to him.

The help of the Commissioners of the R.C.A. & H.M.S. is also sincerely acknowledged for allowing us to incorporate information from ARGYLL Volumes 6 & 7 – particularly for permission to see and use Vol. 7 before publication. I am also extremely grateful for permission to reproduce Figures 1–7 and Figures 9–13. All of these are the copyright of the R.C.A. & H.M.S.

I also wish to thank Mr Lionel Masters of Glasgow University, Dept. of Adult and Continuing Education and Mr Alistair Campbell of Airds, Unicorn Pursuivant – for verifying information written about their respective fields of knowledge – Archaeology and Genealogy.

Thanks are also very gratefully given to my many friends in Cowal Archaeological and Historical Society, especially the late Mr Archibald MacIntyre. They have contributed information and many of the Society have proofread the manuscript.

E. B. R.

PREFACE

This book is the second edition of a publication of the early 1970s written by Mairi Paterson under the auspices of the Cowal Archaeological Society. It was entitled *Cowal Before History* and dealt only with the prehistoric period. Since then new monuments have been discovered, excavation has revealed new evidence and archaeological thinking has progressed. The Society – renamed the Cowal Archaeological and Historical Society considers that 1993 is the opportune time to re-publish and enlarge the book bringing the story of Cowal up to modern times.

As the present book is based on the format of the first, the present editor is indebted to Mairi Paterson for the initial hard work of creating the early edition.

Cowal is a peninsula of about 67,000 hectares lying NE-SW between Loch Fyne and Loch Long which opens into the Firth of Clyde. It is approximately 32 miles (51km) long by 8 miles (13km) broad. The mountains of the northern end rise to 900m and here there are neither roads nor arable land. The southern end is deeply cut by fiords and glens which run far into the hills. The hills rise to a maximum of 500m but are mostly under 300m with low lying ground bordering the shore and in the glens.

As will be seen from the distribution maps, from the second millennium onwards the occupation of the west and east of Cowal appears to be markedly different. This contrast is discussed in the chapter on the Roman period. When documented history first begins in the 12th–13th centuries AD this variant is again marked as the Clyde shore and its hinterland appear to be under the control of the great families of central Scotland while the west is owned by Irish-related families.

It is strongly recommended that Ordnance Survey maps are used by anyone wishing to visit the sites. The best maps to use are the Pathfinder Series (1:25,000) and about ten of them are needed to cover the entire area. Only four – sheets 55, 56, 62, and 63 – of the 1:50,000 scale are required.

It cannot be too strongly emphasised, however, that the sites are all on private ground and the nearest farm, house or forestry office should always be contacted to ask permission before setting off across the hill. This applies even if the site is marked by an asterisk in the gazetteers.

I would also emphasise that anyone crossing the hills, moorlands, or meadows should obey the countryside code implicitly, viz., leave no litter, leave gates as you find them, keep dogs under control and if sheep or cattle are about do not take dogs at all. Finally, the monuments should not be disturbed in any way as significant evidence could be destroyed unwittingly. If anything of interest is found please report it to the address at the end of the book.

FIGURES

MAPS

This book is dedicated to
the late Dorothy N. Marshall
without whose inspiration and enthusiasm
there would have been no
Cowal Archaeological & Historical Society
and thus no book.

INTRODUCTION

PALAEOLITHIC PERIOD
Before 7,000 BC

It is difficult, when we look at the green shores of the Firth of Clyde today, to visualise this part of Scotland 24,000 years ago, at the height of the last great Ice Age when the northern part of Britain was covered by a vast layer of ice. We know, however, from the deep, glacier-carved lochs, such as Loch Eck, and the huge striated boulders still lying where the moving ice left them, that this area was once so completely covered by the great ice cap that no human life was possible. Only the south coast of England escaped the most serious effects of the Ice Ages and only there have traces of Paleolithic (Early Stone Age) Man been found.

About 10,000 years ago the ice began to recede and warmer weather allowed the growth of forests of birch and pine. As a result some animal life spread northwards and with it came people. Evidence of human activity has been found in Yorkshire, and on the Island of Rhum as early as 6,500 BC.

MESOLITHIC PERIOD
c. 7,000 BC to 4,000 BC

The people who came then to Scotland were food gatherers. They lived mainly on easily caught game, on berries, nuts, seaweeds, fish and shellfish. They did not settle in one place but would move according to the seasons and food supply, probably returning to known sites year after year. The sites – though not all as early as the above dates – are primarily recognised by surface collections of tiny worked flints and sometimes by untidy mounds of empty shells – middens. They are always around the shore line, at the heads of sea lochs and often near to the mouths of rivers. The shore line was of course different from today as the sea level has changed and so in some flat areas the sites are quite far inland, as at the Shewelton flats near Irvine. At that time all of the land unless it was waterlogged would be clothed with forest up to about 1,000 ft. The Hunter/Gatherers had little inclination to destroy the woodland though it is now thought that they may have either deliberately or accidentally burned areas of forest. However their main interest was the seashore and the banks of rivers.

Their sites have been found in Jura, Oronsay, Islay, Ayrshire and Galloway but so far no Mesolithic sites have been found in Cowal. Nevertheless the name 'Shellfield' – a farm by the side of Loch Riddon – has an old name translated from the Gaelic. It suggests the presence of mounds of shells and the location, like many others around the head of the sealochs, would be attractive to the Hunter-Gatherers. All shell mounds however do not belong to Mesolithic times.

THE NEOLITHIC PERIOD
Between c. 4,000 BC and c. 2,300 BC

The Mesolithic peoples who clustered in little groups along the western coast of Scotland were nomadic hunters and food gatherers. While they lived in their caves or rock shelters, people in the Middle East – Anatolia and Palestine – were discovering that plants could be grown where they were needed and animals could be herded and cared for rather than simply hunted. The knowledge that crops could be grown and animals domesticated made all future progress possible. These two steps meant that people could live settled lives and form stable communities; they meant the growth of society and of some form of organisation to control it; they meant that particular families became the guardians of particular areas of land and they meant that the invention of new skills, such as the making of pottery, of weaving and eventually of metal working became possible.

The method of farming they practised seems both primitive and wasteful today. They cleared the ground, probably by burning, and cultivated it with hoes or digging sticks. They knew nothing of rotation of crops and gradually exhausted the fertility of the ground. When the crops became too poor to support the community these early farmers moved on to find new land to till. In the course of thousands of years this gradual expansion led these Neolithic peoples round the shores of the Mediterranean, up the western coasts of Europe and through the Danube basin until they or their ideas had colonised almost the whole of Europe. They reached Scotland about 6,000 years ago, probably both from across the North Sea and from the South by Ireland and the Irish Sea.

We know little of the way these people lived for their houses – probably made of wood and turf – have long since disappeared. But at Skara Brae in Orkney the homes of one community are still to be seen, complete with beds, dressers, cupboards and food containers. Because of the shortage of wood in that area, the houses and 'furniture' had been made of stone and thus survive. Stone and bone tools also survive

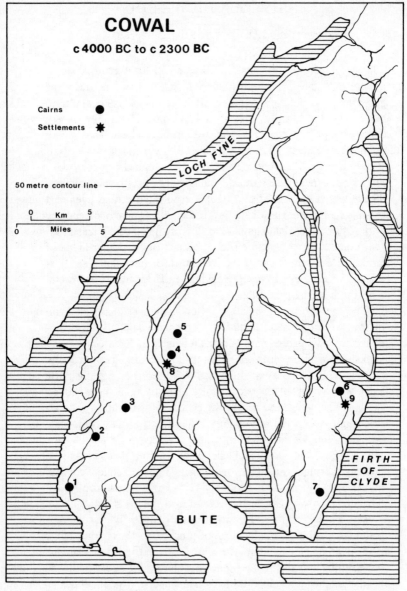

COWAL
c 4000 BC to c 2300 BC

Cairns   ●

Settlements   ✴

50 metre contour line   ———

LOCH FYNE

5

4

8

3

2

6

9

1

7

FIRTH OF CLYDE

BUTE

1. Neolithic cairns and domestic sites

but tools and possessions which they must also have poss-
essed, made of wood, leather and fibre, have disappeared.
Recently however much has been learned from wetland
archaeology. In Central Europe corduroy roads, house
timbers and the small perishable utensils of people of the 5th
and 4th millennia BC have been preserved under water and in
bogland (Coles, 1989). These give us an insight into the way
of life of Neolithic Man.

In Cowal two sites where these Neolithic peoples lived have
been found. One is on the ground of Ardnadam/Dunloskin
(9) 1 mile north of Dunoon (Rennie, 1983); the other at
Auchategan, Glendaruel (8) immediately above the hotel
(Marshall, 1977). The occupation of both of these sites is
dated to before 3,000 BC. In both, post holes, hearths, floors,
stone tools and sherds of pottery were found under a series of
levels dating from the Early Neolithic to the Medieval period.
At Auchategan the number of post holes found was not
sufficient to show the outline of the house. But at Ardnadam
at least three sub-rectangular houses stood on the ground
beside the burn and a round house was on the hillside above.

At Ardnadam two periods of Neolithic occupation were
uncovered with nearly 1,000 years separating them. The
earlier was dated by the carbon taken from the hearth; the later
by the broken pot which had been washed off the floor by
flooding. The pot was judged by a pottery expert to date to
the Late Neolithic Period, c. 2,300 BC.

The only relics of the Neolithic period which remain above
ground and are visible without excavation are the great stone
burial mounds. They are found all over N. and W. Scotland,
in England, Ireland and all along the West coast of Europe.
They are described as family burial vaults and certainly they
were so used for many generations. However, latter day
thinking considers that eventually they became territorial
markers into which some of the bones of the leaders were
placed. It is thought that each area of land which was farmed
and occupied by a particular family or clan had its own tomb
and it was enlarged to become a great cairn built on a
conspicuous hill where it could be seen by all around.

Recent excavation and thinking suggests that the earliest of the tombs were simple boxes built with large slabs of stone set on edge with a capstone as a lid. These are called 'cists'. As the centuries passed, and new ideas evolved, other boxes were added to the original one and thus, as the number of boxes doubled and sometimes trebled, the tomb was enlarged. Eventually, forecourts were added to enhance the entrances and to give arenas for ritual ceremonies. Sometimes long tails of stone were added at the opposite end from the entrance. Finally these great tombs were made even more impressive by covering the whole with a mound of smaller stones to form a cairn.

A Neolithic cairn at Crarae, on Loch Fyne side is estimated to have been 115 feet by 60 feet, with three internal burial chambers, and a flattened forecourt. Unfortunately, most of these cairns are in ruins, as they provided a useful quarry for road making or dyke building, and in many cases only the slabs of the burial chamber remain.

Six Neolithic cairns and a doubtful seventh are known in Cowal. Two of them – Ardachearanbeg (5) and Ardnadam (6) – are probably early as they are simple box tombs. The others have forecourts and 'tails' and so they may have been updated over the centuries. Ardnadam (6) and Lephinkill (4) may be the family tombs associated with the two Neolithic domestic sites mentioned above as each is within half a mile of the living area. The seventh is doubtful as it may be Late Neolithic in date or later. It is described in the following gazetteer under 'Innellan' (7). It is very probable that there may have been other cairns which have been destroyed over the centuries.

Neolithic Sites

Cairns

ARG numbers in brackets refer to Henshall, 1972.
(Only those sites marked with an asterisk are sufficiently preserved to be worth visiting.)

1.   ***Ardmarnoch (ARG. 17)**
     NR 916 726
A few hundred yards S.E. of Ardmarnoch House are the ruins of a megalithic cist lying at the N.E. end of an even more

ruinous cairn. The whole structure was very overgrown with rhododendrons but the cist was uncovered a few years ago and will remain visible until the undergrowth is once again dense. The cist is spectacular having high sides and two large portal stones.

2. *Ach-na-ha, Kilfinan (ARG. 14)
NR 932 817

This impressive cairn is now surrounded by and hidden from the road by a forestry plantation. It lies 150m east of the road – B8000 – one mile south of the hairpin junction of the Otter Ferry/Glenaruel hill road and the B8000. The crescentic forecourt and burial chambers are in good state of preservation but the cairn was removed over 200 years ago possibly to build the surrounding dykes. The single standing stone to the S.W. may mark the limit of the original cairn. One of the stones of the forecourt has been 'sanctified', probably in Medieval times, by having a cross incised on it.

3. Carn Ban, Glendaruel
NR 952 839

This is considered by some of the experts to be a very denuded long chambered cairn. It was classified as such about 50 years ago but since then has become so overgrown that it was not recognised and as a result was damaged by forestry ploughing. It is within 200m of the Otter Ferry/Glendaruel hill road, overlooking Loch Fyne, within the forestry fence on the N. side of the burn gorge.

4. Lephinkill, Glendaruel (ARG. 16)
NS 002 843

140m above and to the East of the hotel in Glendaruel and now surrounded by forestry plantation is the Cairn which may be associated with Neolithic occupation of Auchategan. The cairn was only discovered in 1964. It was then recognised as a mound of stone 80ft long with a crescentic forecourt facing to the N.E. Now, as the animals no longer graze the ground, grass and heather have overgrown the mound and enveloped the forecourt and the monument is no longer recognisable.

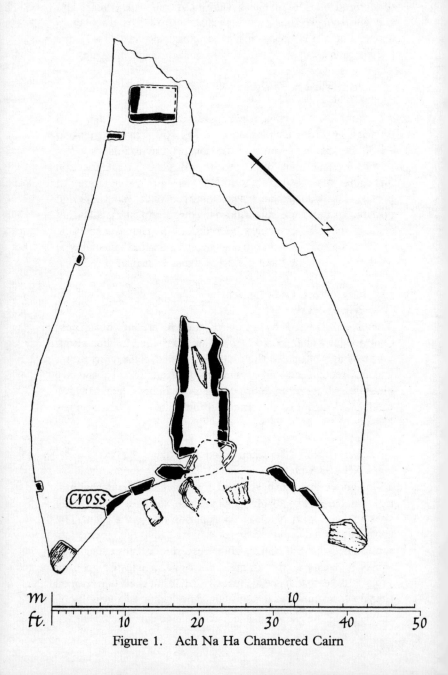

Figure 1. Ach Na Ha Chambered Cairn

5. Ardachearanbeg, Glendaruel (ARG. 15)
NS 005 852

1km due north of Lephinkill Cairn on the same contour there
is a small Neolithic cairn with the burial chamber exposed. It
is now surrounded by forestry plantation but, although the site
itself is preserved, it may be difficult to locate as the vegetation
will have engulfed it. It is very probable that this is an early
tomb and may pre-date the large one to the south – No. 4.

6. *'Adam's Grave', Ardnadam (ARG. 18)
NS 161 800

This is a much denuded burial cairn which can be seen on the
west of the Dunoon/Sandbank road just north of Sandbank
School. It is situated near Ardnadam farm. All of the cairn
material has been removed, leaving the great stones of the
chamber visible. This cairn may be the tomb associated with
the Neolithic domestic site – Ardnadam, NS 163 791 – which
is situated under the power lines 1 km to the south.

7. *The Tom, Innellan
NS 149 715

The period to which this cairn belongs is doubtful. It is
suggested that it may be a transitional type between the
Neolithic and the Bronze ages, i.e. perhaps belonging to the
period around 2,000 BC. It was discovered in 1990 by the
forestry workers in preparation for extracting timber. It is a
small crescentic shaped cairn with an arc of six upstanding
slabs of stone forming an apparent forecourt within and
against the inner curve of the arc.

It stands at about 200m O.D. above Knockamillie Castle
and can be approached by the forestry roads. At the time of
going to press the cairn is covered by polythene and topsoil to
preserve it during the felling operations.

Settlement sites

8. Auchategan, Glendaruel (Marshall, 1977: pp. 36–74)
NS 000 843

The Auchategan domestic site is on a natural shelf 40m below
the Lephinkill Cairn overlooking the hotel. It was fully

excavated in the late 1960s and so nothing visible remains. Forestry trees were planted over the entire area. Enough post holes were found to show that two huts, at least, had stood on the ground in a first period. At a later period the hearths and post holes of more huts, pottery and flint tools overlay the first occupation. This occupation was dated to the early 3rd millennium BC.

9.   Ardnadam, Dunoon. (Rennie, 1984: pp. 13–22)
NS 163 791

Two main periods of Neolithic occupation were found within the Enclosure at Ardnadam. The earlier consisted of at least three sub-rectangular houses, hearths, working areas, pottery and stone tools. This occupation was dated to the late 4th millennium BC (See Plan 12). About 1,000 years later a round house was built overlying two of the earlier houses. From it came so many sherds of a large pot that it was possible to reconstruct it. The pot is now in the Hunterian Museum in Glasgow.

NS 163 789 (Rennie – forthcoming)

On the hill above the Enclosure under much later levels the post holes and floor of another Neolithic House was excavated. It had been a round timber-framed structure with a central hearth. A flint scraper was found amongst the carbon of the hearth. This hut was also dated by the carbon to the late 4th millennium BC.

THE BRONZE AGE

Between c. 2,300 BC and c. 700 BC

As the discovery of farming caused the wandering Hunter/ Gatherers to settle down and live in the one area, the discovery that metals could be used to make more efficient tools may have accelerated and magnified the change from an egalitarian to an hierarchical society.

When the art of working metal was discovered copper and gold were first used for ornaments. Copper was eventually utilised for weapons, but not to any great extent, until it was discovered that by the addition of tin a new stronger metal was formed – bronze. Central Europe and the Iberian Peninsula appear to have been the main centres of diffusion of bronze weapons but the metal workers travelled far in search of their raw materials. The result of this was the growth of trade and barter and the spread of new ideas and techniques. Some families being more astute than others profited more from the interchange of goods and theories and thus became more powerful – chiefs, ruling families, allegiance to the tribe and the antithesis, slavery, may have been initiated.

Archaeologists now doubt that waves of migrating people were the source of the knowledge of metal working. The more recent thought is that the skill and knowledge of making bronze was carried by single craftsmen who came practising their techniques and looking for patronage. Nevertheless, a new shape of pottery vessel – Beakers – and a new way of burial – Cists – was introduced about the same time as the first copper weapons. Because these Beakers are frequently found in the cist burials sometimes with copper weapons it is still debated whether or not there was a large-scale immigration or simply the transference of ideas by traders and lone craftsmen. Beakers are a particular shape of vessel thought to have contained a beer-like drink made from the distillation of wild flowers, herbs and barley. Cists are small box-like graves used to inter a single crouched body.

By this time the use of the great chambered tombs had become obsolete. The form of burial now reflects a stratified

society. It would appear that the greater the chief or leader –
the greater was the cairn that covered his personal grave.
Throughout the transitional period cists were sometimes
inserted into the sides of the cairns of the earlier chambered
tombs. Afterwards cists were sunk directly into the ground
sometimes with no overlying cairn but sometimes with
covering round cairns of varying sizes presumably depending
upon the importance of the person whose remains were
buried underneath. Frequently the dead were accompanied by
their weapons, by personal ornaments or even by a Beaker
with liquid refreshment. Elaborate necklaces of jet or lignite
were found in the Glebe Cairn at Kilmartin and in a cist burial
on the island of Inchmarnock off Bute. Later still, well into the
2nd millennium BC, the practice of cremation seems to have
become accepted. The ashes of the dead were then put into
cinerary urns – a vessel rather like a Beaker – and it was either
put into a cist or set directly into the ground.

In Cowal there are or have been many round burial cairns
and probably many more single cists. These are listed in the
following gazetteer (Plan 2). Two however are of particular
interest because of their size and position – the 20m cairn at
200m on top of the crags at Evanachen (11) and the other
20m round cairn at 300m above Strone farm, Otter Ferry
(10). Who were the chieftains buried high above Loch Fyne
under these cairns and where did they live?

Until comparatively recently little was known about the
domestic sites of the Bronze Age people. Over the last twenty
years this has changed, as forestry ploughing has exposed and
allowed for the excavation of many Bronze Age Round houses
on Arran. Bronze Age houses have also been recognised in
Renfrewshire and on the island of Islay. Unfortunately, in
Cowal none of the round foundations known can claim to be
as early as Bronze Age. Yet the houses must have been here
and their post holes must remain somewhere, as yet
undiscovered under the turf.

Significantly, the known Bronze Age monuments – Round
Cairns, Standing Stones and Cup and Ring Scribings – cluster
around the Kilfinan, Ardmarnoch and Ardlamont areas on the
E. side of Loch Fyne. This is an area where copper occurs

naturally in the ground and even more significantly, it is the area across Loch Fyne from the Kilmartin region – a region pre-eminent in Bronze Age times. Thus, in this district on east Loch Fyneside there must be 2nd millennium settlements.

Plans 3 & 4 show the position of the 2nd millennium monuments. The remains of only one stone circle can still be seen in Cowal. It is, interestingly, at the cross roads in Kames (17) suggesting rather that the cross roads are at 'the Stones'. There was at one time a circle of twelve stones in Strachur Bay (14) on what is now the lawn in front of Strachur House. Until recently one stone still stood upright but even that has now gone. The tendency for upright stones to collapse particularly after the passage of 3,000 years makes it surprising that so many still remain. About ten singles or pairs and one group of three, can be seen.

The pair of stones at Stillaig Farm (18 & 9) illustrate one of the interpretations suggested to explain the presence of Standing Stones whether as singles, pairs, lines, or circles. The two stones at Stillaig are 500m apart and, together with a particular hill across Loch Fyne in Knapdale, it is said they form a lunar observatory. In other areas stone settings are thought to mark the rising or setting of the sun or of a particular star at a specified day in the year. In theory the explanation seems logical as all agricultural communities had to have a calendar to tell them when to start each farming activity. The rising of the sun or particular star over a known landmark when seen from the same point year after year would give that signal. However, except in some obviously visible cases it is difficult for twentieth-century man or woman to translate the theory into the landscape of today particularly as many of the stones have collapsed and the panoramic view has changed.

Other simpler explanations which probably have some truth in them are that the standing stones are the markers for burials, the landmarks for seafarers, phallic symbols or the centre piece for fertility rituals. The circles are also postulated as arenas for fertility rites, or as tribal gathering places, and/or even as trading and bartering sites. It is possible that all of these explanations were valid at different times.

The cup-marked scribings have a wide variety of

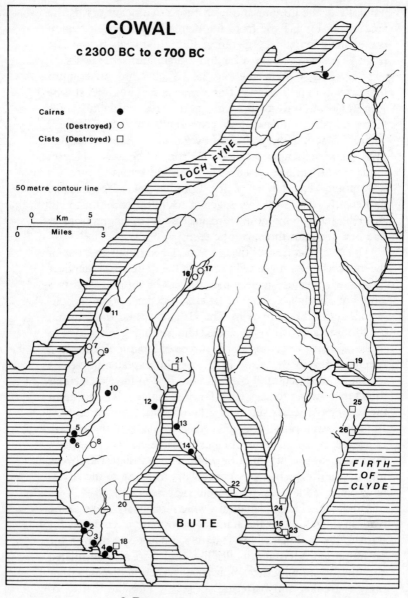

COWAL

c 2300 BC to c 700 BC

Cairns ●
(Destroyed) ○
Cists (Destroyed) □

50 metre contour line ——

2. Bronze age cairns and cists

explanations attributed to them, evidence that we are still far from understanding such strange symbols. The marks consist of small, shallow cups, often about 5cm diameter and 2cm deep. They are cut into rock outcrops, boulders and standing stones or other built monuments, such as cists. They occur singly or in groups and are sometimes encircled with concentric rings or a single ring. The Kilmartin area is rich in these symbols and a rock face there at Achnabrec Farm one mile N.W. of Lochgilphead is worth a visit. There the concentric circles frequently number up to ten and twelve around a cup and spread to nearly one metre on the rock face. In Cowal there is nothing as spectacular as these but single cups and groups of cups are common. Explanations given are that they are associated with copper prospecting, that they are star maps, route maps, family trees, or containers for blood at sacrifices! None of which really sound credible – it is difficult for modern man brought up with computers, television and food arriving by petrol-engine transport to think with the mind of 3,000 years ago.

Until very recently Cup marks were considered to date from the 2nd millennium when metal was first being worked and used, thus they are so classified in this book. However, this dating is now disputed and present thought considers that Rock Scribings belong to later Neolithic times. When found on later monuments such as cists it is argued that the stones have been re-used.

Throughout the country authentic evidence is sometimes found of the presence 4,000 years ago of the wandering metal workers. The evidence is the discovery of the smith's stock – his raw materials and the objects he has made. Such a find was made when the garden of Ballimore House near Otter Ferry was being landscaped around 1900 (26). Buried in the ground there were seven spearheads, eight bronze axes, two swords and a corrugated bronze tube. The spearheads and swords were broken or were not complete; the axes were of the Irish type. It is thought that this hoard had been deliberately buried and was probably meant to be recovered.

Bronze Age Sites

Round Cairns (Still visible or known to have existed)

Sites marked with an asterisk are preserved and worth visiting.

1. **Ardno, Cairndow**
    *NN 156 080

In the triangle of ground to the south of the junction of the Hell's Glen road (B839) with the A886, there is a cairn with an open cist set into it. The cap stone is lost but the four sides of the cist form a large rectangular box 2m by 1m by 0.9m in depth. The surrounding cairn is 10m in diameter and about 2m high.

2. **Port-a-Mhadaidh** (Three cairns have been recorded in this area)
    NR 930 698

To the N.E. of the abandoned construction site, and 550m N. of Port-a-Mhadaidh farm to the S. of the burn there is a grass-covered mound about 10m in diameter and 0.9m in height.

   NR 929 694

To the N.W. of the farm there is a mound 6m by 5m which is traditionally said to be a burial-place.

   NR 933 691

Situated 350m E.S.E. of the farm now under the road there is a cairn 6m in diameter. It was excavated in advance of the widening of the road and was found to have a kerbed inner core 4.5m in diameter, enclosed by an outer kerb.

3. **Stillaig Bay**
    *NR 932 675

A large cairn situated on the machair ground above Port Leathen and 100m to the W. of the track has been greatly disturbed in the past. It is 17m in diameter and still stands 1.5m high though the centre has been severely robbed. 20m to the S. there is a small oval mound 3m x 4m.

4. **Asgog Bay**
   *NR 943 677

Two cairns are situated E. of the burn that runs into the bay and about 200m from the high tide mark. The more northerly is 17m in diameter and 1.8m high; the more southerly about 14m diameter and 1m high. In the larger cairn which was excavated in 1927 there was a small cist containing a Food Vessel. The smaller one has been severely robbed and only the rim remains.

5. **Fearnoch Farm, Kilfinan**
   *NR 926 793

In the field, 300m S. of the farmhouse there is a grass covered round cairn, 15m in diameter and 1.2m in height.

6. **Fearnoch Farm, Kilfinan**
   *NR 924 790

Another severely denuded cairn is situated on the S. side of the Kilfinan burn 75m E. of the footbridge. It measures about 8m diameter and is 0.5m in height.

7. **Kilail, Otter Ferry** (Destroyed)
   NR 934 843

It is recorded that a cairn of 'considerable size' was destroyed from the N. bank of the Kilail Burn about 100m to the S. of the farm.

8. **Lindsaig Farm** (Destroyed)
   NR 936 803

This cairn which was recorded as being 8.5m diameter is now engulfed by a forestry plantation and was severely damaged during ploughing.

9. **Kilail, Otter Ferry** (Destroyed)
   NR 944 841

A small cairn only 2m in diameter and 0.3m in height is situated to the N.W. of Barr nam Manach. It was considered to be a cairn as kerbstones are visible on all sides except the north. It is now probably ploughed out by new afforestation.

10. Strone Farm, Otter Ferry
*NR 952 826

Situated on the skyline immediately W. of the forestry
boundary fence at 290m O.D. there is a grass and heather-
covered cairn. It is about 13m in diameter and 1.7m high with
the suggestion of kerbstones on the S.W. arc. The view from
it is extensive to the S. and W. It can be approached from near
to the W. summit of the Otter Ferry/Glendaruel hill road.

11. Evanachan Farm, Otter Ferry
*NR 953 879

On the summit of Creag Evanachan, (195m) there is a large
stone cairn 18m in diameter and standing 2m high. There are
extensive views from it in all directions. It is best approached
from Evanachan Farm where the old Loch Fyneside road can
be followed for most of the way.

12. Lochhead, Loch Riddon
*NR 001 809

A round cairn which only recently has been recognised is set
between two hillslopes above the N.W. side of Loch Riddon.
The cairn has been greatly disturbed centrally but the kerbing
is almost complete. It can be reached by climbing up through
the wood 200m south of the house at the side of the loch.

13. Feorline Farm, Colintraive
NS 015 790

This probable cairn is now lost under a carpet of dead bracken
and is difficult to find. It was recorded as being 3.5m in
diameter and kerbed for 270°.

14. Colintraive
*NS 032 744

In an arable field 100m S.S.W. of Colintraive Hotel is a large
grass-covered cairn set on a stony platform which stands
about 1m above the level of the field. The cairn measures 13m
by 12m and stands 1m in height. A cup-and-ring marked slab
which was found nearby may have come from the cairn.

15.   **Ardyne, Toward** (Destroyed)
      NS 09 68
Just N. of Ardyne Point, under the present site of the oilrig construction yard an immense cairn of stones was removed in 1806.

16.   **Garvie, Glendaruel** (Destroyed) Carn Mor
      NS 034 904
About 150 years ago a large cairn (dimensions not given) was
removed from the flat ground beside the river 200m W.S.W.
of Garvie Farm. The workmen discovered 'five Stone Coffins'
four of which contained urns filled with ashes and the fifth –
human bones.

17.   **Garvie, Glendaruel** (Destroyed) Carn Beag
      NS 036 905
A smaller cairn was destroyed about 200 years ago, from the
ground 100m N. of Garvie. This was probably under the line
of the present road. In it two stone coffins were found each
containing urns filled with ashes.

Cists

18.   **Asgog Bay**
      NR 943 677/NR 943 679
No trace now remains.

19.   **Graham's Point, Kilmun**
      NR 175 812
Three cists recorded but no trace remains.

20.   **Kames**
      NR 973 713
Three cists recorded in 1870; two were about 150m S.E. of
the standing stone in the hedge, the third about 60m N. of the
stone. Other cists were mentioned as being found 'in and
around' Tighnabruaich. No trace remains.

21.   **Auchategan, Glendaruel**
      NS 000 843
In the course of the excavation at this site two cists were

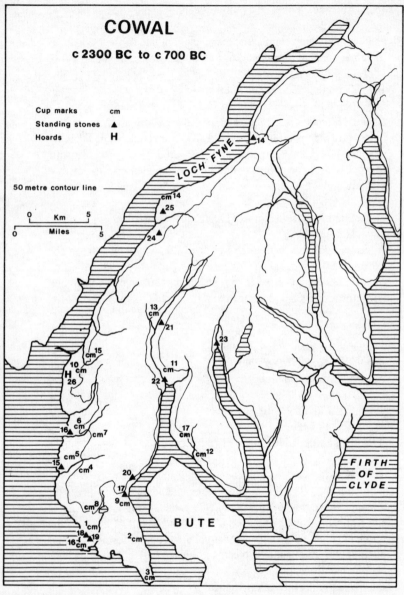

COWAL

c 2300 BC to c 700 BC

Cup marks   cm
Standing stones ▲
Hoards   H

50 metre contour line ——

0   Km   5
0   Miles   5

LOCH FYNE

▲14

cm 14
▲25

24 ▲

13
cm
▲21

23
▲

15
cm
11
cm
10
cm
H
26

22 ▲

6
cm
16 ▲
cm7

17
cm

15
cm5
cm4

cm12

20 ▲
17
▲
9 cm

FIRTH
OF
CLYDE

cm8

1
cm
18 ▲ 19
16 ▲
cm

2
cm

B U T E

3
cm

3. Bronze age cup and ring markings and standing stones

discovered associated with a large area of burning and a crescentic shaped cairn all overlying the Neolithic deposits and underlying a level dated to 660 AD (Marshall, 1977–78).

22. South Hall, Colintraive
NS 059 718
Stone coffins were found in a field on the N. side of the road about 200m. S.S.W. of South Hall House.

23. Ardyne, Toward
NS 09 68
At the beginning of the nineteenth century various cists of differing sizes and descriptions were uncovered near to the large cairn noted in item 13.

24. Knockdow, Toward
NS 104 704
Around 1840 several stone cists containing human bones were uncovered about 250m S. of Knockdown. This point must be quite near to the present road.

25. Ardnadam, Dunoon
NS 163 791
Overlying the Neolithic levels at this site, a possible cist was found which was associated with a cairn-like feature and a hearth. (Rennie, 1984).

26. Dunoon
NS 175 763
Two stone cists are recorded as having been found to the south of the Castle hill at Dunoon, i.e. immediately above the shore at the extreme east end of the West Bay.

Cup-and-Ring Markings

ARG. numbers in brackets refer to Morris, 1977. The markings are so numerous that only some of the most spectacular ones have been listed below.

Those scribings which are most easily found and the Stones which are worth a visit are marked with an asterisk.

1.   **Stillaig, Millhouse**
      *NR 942 683. 942 682, 941 683, 942 683

These four groups of cupmarks are on rock outcrops in pasture
fields about 350m S. of Stillaig farmhouse. Permission to visit
and directions can be requested at the farm.

2.   **Achadachoun, Ardlamont**
      NR 982 673

Immediately W. of the abandoned farmstead of Achadachoun
there is a rectangular slab with fifteen cups. The slab rests
against the E. side of a ruined building.

3.   **Point Farm, Ardlamont (ARG 72)**
      *NR 991 643

300m S.E. of Point Farmhouse, immediately to the E. of the
track and to the S. of a stone dyke, there is an erratic boulder.
On it are eighteen plain cup marks and ten with single rings.

4.   **Auchalick Wood, Ardmarnoch (ARG 10)**
      NR 919 740, 921 740

The first group is on the edge of a slight terrace immediately
above the road. There is a boulder with five cups and two rings,
six cups with single rings and some fifty-nine plain cupmarks.

      The second outcrop lies in a dense forestry plantation but
the scribings are deeply incised. There are six cups with single
rings all with gutters and upwards of eleven plain cupmarks.

5.   **Inveryne, Kilfinan**
      *NR 921 757

On a low rock-sheet 3m E. of the track, there are at least sixty-
three cupmarks.

6.   **Fearnoch, Kilfinan**
      NR (1)926 798, (2)918 800, (3)920 801, (4)921 803

At (1) there are eight cups on a rock outcrop 150m N.W. of
Fearnoch farmhouse. At (2) in rough pasture 960m N.W. of
the farmhouse there is a boulder with seven cupmarks. (3) is
a rock outcrop 230m E. of (2) with three cups and (4) is
260m N.N.E. of (3). It has four cupmarks.

7. Lindsaig, Kilfinan (general N.G.R.) (ARG 62a)
NR 934 795

On the ground which was originally part of Lindsaig Farm there are nine sets of cup mark scribings known. Some of the groups are now under forest and will be difficult to locate. One group is on a boulder lying on level ground within an area of rig-and-furrow cultivation 680m N.E. of the farmhouse – NR 940797. On the boulder are six plain cups and two dumb-bell markings.

8. Derybruich, Millhouse
NR 937 703

A boulder immediately S. of the path from Millhouse to Derybruich and about 150m E. of the cottage at Derybruich there is a boulder with at least thirty-one cupmarks and a faint single-ringed cup.

9. Kames Golf Course
NR 972 708, 972 709, 973 708

These three groups are found on the flanks of Cnoc a'Chuilinn about 200m S.E. of Kames Golf Course clubhouse. The first two groups are cut into rock outcrops, the third is cut into a boulder.

10. Corra, Otter Ferry
NR 936 839

150m E. of the hairpin junction of the Otter Ferry/Glendaruel hill road with the B8000 and 200m N.E. of Corra House within a pasture field but close to the wood, there is a boulder with ten plain cupmarks on it.

11. Glendaruel (ARG 62)
NR 998 840

100m S.E. of the road bridge (A886) over the Clachan Burn in a recent deciduous plantation there is a boulder with ten cupmarks, one of which is surrounded by a single ring and another by a keyhole-shaped ring.

12.   Colintraive. (ARG 81)
NS 033 745

A boulder with two cups, one surrounded by four rings and
the other by three rings, was found in the demolition debris of
the old inn at Colintraive – now the site of the community hall.
The boulder is now housed in the Bute Museum in Rothesay.
It may have come originally from the cairn in the field 150m
to the S.W.

13.   Kildalven, Glendaruel
*NS (1)017 889, (2)013 886, (3)009 883

(1) On a boulder a little to the S.E. of the township there are
twelve plain cups and a pair of conjoined cups.
(2) About 500m to the S.W. on a boulder which is a landmark,
there are twenty-nine plain cups and one dumb-bell marking.
(3) On the first crest of the hill above and to the N.E. of Achanelid Farm there are several rock outcrops. On the highest of
these at about 110m O.D. there are at least twenty-four cups.

14.   Newton Island
NS 034 986

On the S.E. flank of the island and 4m to the E. of the dun
(No. 17) a flat outcrop bears five cupmarks.

15.   Kilail
NS 934 840

Four groups of cupmarks consisting of 4 cups, 18 cups, 11
cups and five cups (one with two probable rings) are on the
flank of the hill Barr nam Manach 1.1km E.S.E. of Kilail
farmhouse.

16.   Low Stillaig
NS 931 679

18 cups are on the upper surface of a boulder N.E. of the
ruins of Low Stillaig.

17.   Ardentraive
NS 035 747

This is a central NGR for three groups of markings which are cut into the crest of a rocky ridge 320m N.N.E. of Ardentraive farmhouse.

Standing Stones and Stone Circles

14. Strachur
NN 089 016
The remaining stone of a postulated circle now lies in a playing-field 90m W.N.W. of Strachur House.

15. Inveryne, Kilfinan
*NR 915 749
These three stones form a linear setting about 200m N.E. of hightide mark in Auchlick Bay and 800m S.W. of the farm. They are all about 1m in height and the same in width. A fourth stone which might have been associated with the setting was disturbed by the plough some years ago. It lay 0.2m below the ground surface and about 15-20m N.W. of the alignment. It was about the same size as the others. It now lies on the grass bank at the side of the field.

16. Fearnoch, Kilfinan
*NR 926 793
This is a massive stone 1.95m in greatest width and standing 2.5m high. It is incorporated into a dyke 400m S. of Fearnoch farm. It is about 90m S.W. of the cairn No. 5.

17. Kames Crossroads
*NR 971 714
Three standing stones remain of a possible circle where the roads at Kames intersect. The largest – 2.8m in height – is set in a bank and hedge at the N.E. corner. A smaller stone is beside it. The third stone is within the enclosure of the War Memorial at the S.W. corner.

18. Low Stillaig, Millhouse
*NR 931 683
Two stones stand in open moorland halfway between the derelict construction village of Pollphail and Low Stillaig farmhouse. One stone stands 2.9m high; the other has been

broken and is represented by the stump. It is said that the broken part was used as a lintel for a byre at Low Stillaig. These two stones are considered to be associated with the single stone at Creag Loisgte, Low Stillaig.

19.   Creag Loisgte, Low Stillaig
      *NR 935 677

Immediately to the N.W. of the road leading to Port Leathan and 550m E. of Low Stillaig there is a single quadrangular stone standing 1.9m high. The 2.9m stone on the moor 550m to the N.W. can be seen on the skyline.

20.   Tighnabruaich
      NR 981 731

Immediately within the entrance to Tighnabruaich House there is a standing stone 2m in height.

21.   Ardachearanbeg, Glendaruel
      NS 002 861

On a terrace overlooking the River Ruel, 260m N. of Ardachearanbeg there is a single stone 1.5m in height and 1m by 0.2 at the base. It has slanting sides rising to a point.

22.   Auchnagarron, Loch Riddon
      NS 006 821

200m S.S.W. of the farm, in pasture land, there is a 1m stone measuring about 4.15m in girth at the base. Another stone, across the river in the adjoining field, was overthrown some years ago.

23.   Balliemore, Loch Striven
      *NS 056 845

Two standing stones about 2m apart stand in a level field about 140m S. of the farm. The stones are different in character – one being a thin slab 2.44m high; the other is a block about 1.65m high.

24. Barnacarry, Strathlachlan
NS 004 944

This stone cannot now be found although it appears to have been known as recently as 1940. The name 'Barnacarry' comes from a standing stone – presumably this lost one.

25. Portindrain, Strathlachlan
NS 013 974

This upright stone may be a 'standing stone'. It stands about 500m W.S.W. of the old township of Portindrain in the N.W. corner of a partial enclosure. It stands 1.5m high by about 0.75m broad but narrows to the top.

Hoard

26. Ballimore House
NR 926 832

In 1912 when the garden to the house was being prepared a hoard of bronze weapons – spearheads, axes and swords – was discovered. All were broken.

THE IRON AGE

Between 700 BC and 500 AD

Both the name and the dates given for the title of this chapter
are ambiguous. The names 'Bronze Age', 'Iron Age' etc. were
applied in the late nineteenth century when thinkers were first
attempting to classify and put into human context the objects
which were being found in the early 'excavations'. The dates
are also exceedingly controversial. No one can give an initial
date for the time when mankind first began to use iron
regularly. The terminating date is also misleading as the
manner of life which characterises the 'Iron Age' continued in
the West of Scotland until 1745. In Europe the span of time
implied by 'Iron Age' is usually equated with the rise and the
period of supremacy of the Celts. In Britain the first intro-
duction of iron may have been made by individual Celtic
'smiths' who crossed to Britain centuries before the tribal
immigration. The first use of iron may have been as presti-
gious personal items made by 'smiths' under the patronage of
particular chiefs.

The Hittites are usually given the credit for having
discovered how to smelt iron from its ores and to make iron
tools but even this is a simplified theory. However, it is
recognised that the smelting and working of iron developed in
the area round the Black Sea probably as early as the 3rd
millennium BC. The first known appearance of iron in central
Europe was abut 700 BC. Iron swords, ploughshares and
knives were brought by warrior horsemen from their
homelands on the grasslands far to the East. These were the
people who were to become known to history as the Celts.

Their iron weapons, their iron tools and their knowledge of
horses gave them such an advantage that they spread over
Europe, overcoming and intermarrying with the earlier
peoples. They ranged and dispersed so much that over the
centuries they split up into various tribes whose names
became associated with particular places and are still in use to
day – Dunkeld, Selkirk, Kent and Paris. The tribes gradually
spread to the west of France, south into what is now Spain

and eventually across the Channel into Britain. As they dispersed, their original language changed into dialects which have come down to us as different forms of Welsh and Gaelic. Other forms such as Gaulish have died out completely.

By the 3rd century BC need for still more land took the Celts across the Alps and brought them into contact with another people who were prospering and spreading around the Mediterranean – the Romans. For about 250 years the Roman Empire expanded and grew by trading with, fighting and overcoming in turn each of the various Celtic tribes, for the Celts never learnt to unite and fight as one people. Eventually the Celts and their homelands from the Black Sea to southern Britain became part of the Roman Empire – all, that is, but Ireland, North Britain and the Scandinavian Countries which were never conquered.

More is known about the way of life of the Celtic race than of the earlier prehistoric peoples. We know of them from contemporary Roman records, from traditional Irish poems and recently from excavation both in Europe and Britain. They were warlike, aggressive, delighting in conflict, but at the same time, patrons of the arts, loving personal adornment and honouring poets and artists. They were a 'warrior aristocracy' with a carefully defined social structure of chiefs, priests, warriors, peasants, and slaves. Their wealth, certainly in the earlier days in Europe and finally in the West, was in their cattle.

The priests, the much-maligned 'Druids', were the custodians of the laws and traditions of the Celtic peoples. Their training for this responsible position was long and arduous for the Celtic laws and customs were handed down by word of mouth. In their own persons the Druids embodied all that was distinctive in the Celtic way of life with a code of law which was almost as detailed and comprehensive as Roman law itself. When the Roman armies invaded Britain the Druids were at the centre of the resistance, and one of the most savage campaigns of the Roman army was fought with the express purpose of destroying the main centre of Druid learning in Anglesey.

Until recently it was thought that the 'Iron Age Forts'

which are so numerous throughout Britain were so called because they were the fortified living places of the Celtic tribes. The implication is that warfare was so endemic that they had to live their lives within the forts. Excavation over the past twenty-five years has qualified this theory; the great multi-ramparted 'forts' of the South of England such as Maiden Castle are now known to be fortified hilltop towns where the agricultural produce of an area was stored and then distributed.

However, the greater number of the inhabitants would live outside of the great fortified enclosure for there the work had to be done to produce the grain for storage and the leather, skins and iron objects for trading. From smaller farm enclosures the animals had to be herded and cared for; the ground had to be tilled and the crops harvested, iron ore had to be extracted from the ground and the woodlands had to be managed for wood was a basic raw material.

Round Iron-Age houses and farms have now been found which are not fortified although they are enclosed by ditches and banks to protect and enclose the animals and the people from wolves and other wild animals. It is now believed that the Round Houses and farms of the ordinary people were widespread throughout the country although evidence of their presence is only found when the ground surface is broken during building operations. The Butser Ancient Farm Project in Hampshire is an experimental replica of an Iron-Age farm built and furnished to attempt to show and to discover how the people lived and worked.

Nevertheless, defence of one's property appears to have become more important in the 1st millennium BC than it was in the earlier Bronze Age. One of the reason is perhaps a change in climate. The weather is known to have deteriorated between 1200 and 600 BC and peat began to form over ground which had previously been intensively farmed. The result was that there was a shortage of usable land.

Secondly, in the last few hundred years BC as the Celtic tribes began to move into the South of Britain, the population grew and the need for more land intensified. Finally, as iron weapons became customary and the Celtic joy in conflict became a national pastime, fear of one's neighbours grew and a fortified refuge for the family and the cattle became a necessity. As the fortified refuges were built of stone and the houses were usually built of timber it is the refuges which have survived and usually the houses are only found through excavation.

In the West of Scotland various forms of fortification are known and a tentative chronology has been suggested though the chronology has now been reduced to only two main types – an earlier and a later and even that division probably overlaps. Hillforts are considered to be the earlier and Duns to be the later. 'Enclosures' in the gazetteer may correspond to the non-fortified farmsteads of the south or, if small in diameter, to be the actual wall-stumps of stone-built isolated round houses. 'Vitrified' forts – an outdated classication – is now regarded as a misnomer and their dating, like that of the Enclosures, is probably across the timespan of the Iron Age.

The early Hillforts may have two or even three enclosing ramparts but none of the Cowal ones has more than one. They may be tribal centres, trading centres, and strongholds and correspond to the great Iron Age Hillforts of the south. Some (the smaller ones) may in fact be the fortified homesteads of a petty ruler although the larger duns could equally have served the same purpose. Different sites may have served at different periods – a time span of 1,000 years is under discussion. In Cowal, the walls of the Hillforts appear to be insignificant, but this may be deceptive as substantial timber palisades may at one time have crowned them. In the following gazetteer eight sites are classified as 'Hillforts' but classification is always arbitrary and likely to be changed by later generations.

The later types of fortified structure are the 'Duns'. They are described as enclosing a smaller area and having much thicker walls. They would appear to be family refuges but it is possible that some may have been occupied continuously – that is, that they were in fact domestic dwellings. The walls are built of dry stone and are usually massive but not always. The Galleried Duns have very massive walls, often 6 to 7m broad. They enclose cells, passages and staircases leading to the wallhead where there may have been a palisade and catwalk.

They are considered to be later than the simple Duns. The simple Duns have less imposing walls though still very broad and built of stone. Eleven sites in Cowal are classified as 'Duns' and three of these are Galleried.

The so-called 'Vitrified Forts' should in reality be termed 'Timber-laced Forts which have been burnt'. Timber-lacing is a form of construction in which timber beams are enclosed within a stone wall – the beams lying vertically, horizontally and along the length. When the beams catch fire either through enemy action or domestic accident the cavity caused by the burning beam forms a flue which raises the temperature within the wall to such an extent that ingredients of the stone melt forming a glassy mass. Timber-laced Forts are known throughout Britain and Europe, some being vitrified, others not.

In the east of Scotland the burnt timber-laced forts – the vitrified ones – were considered to be earlier than the single and double ramparted Hillforts. But, in the west, vitrified enclosures overlie the wall stumps of the large Hillforts showing that these Hillforts are earlier. In Cowal (Plan 4) one of the Hillforts (5) may be timber-laced though not burnt, and three of the duns (11, 16, 19) have been timber-laced and burnt i.e. vitrified. This illustrates the difficulty of dating such sites.

The third classification in the gazetteer – Enclosures – is intentionally a vague term as its criterion is 'a small area enclosed with lightweight walls'. It is possible that many of these may be domestic sites of the Iron Age people, i.e. embanked farmyards. Within them and under the turf the postholes of the round domestic houses, workshops and byres may be found. The site at Ardnadam (27) exemplifies this for within the enclosure the evidence for two Iron Age Houses was discovered. The very small circular areas (20, 26, & 27) may be the foundations of Round Houses without enclosing walls. The Hut Circles – No. 28 – are classified differently as they are so small that they are accepted as hut foundations. Because of the difference it is suggested that they might belong to an earlier period, perhaps Bronze Age – 2nd Millennium BC. Even if the Enclosures are settlement sites common sense advises that the eight described cannot be the complete domestic occupation of Iron Age Cowal. Many enclosures must have been ploughed out, others yet may not have been recognised, but the greater number have probably been built wholly of timber and nothing has remained above ground to indicate their position.

Another type of site at one time thought to be solely associated with the Iron Age are the crannogs. Now they are found to be dated as early as Neolithic and as late as Medieval. (Morrison, 1985). These are artificial islands or sometimes natural islands built or utilised as the sites for round timber-framed houses. These are found in swamps, lochs or tidal estuaries. Recently much archaeological excavation and research has been expended on them. Some are known in Cowal; some are suspected to lie under the lochs; and known islands may yet be discovered to be crannogs as they support round houses.

Dunoon Castle may have been built on an earlier Iron Age refuge as the prefix word 'dun' implies a fortified point. The name of Dunloskin, a farm 1 mile N. of Dunoon, NS 169 780, suggests that this site also may have been defended. The field in front of the house shows some indication of having been banked and ditched but as the ground has probably been ploughed and reaped for 1,000 years little positive evidence can be expected from surface traces. However, the noticeable hill behind the farm also has a name suggesting fortification – 'Dunan' – 'the little fort' ('an' being the diminutive in Gaelic). The implication is that there may have been two forts – a little one and a greater one. This gives more credence to the suggestion that there was a Dun at Dunloskin Farm. On the Dunan Hill no sign of defensive works have been found, but the steepness of the gradient makes walling unnecessary especially if the hill was a look-out point covering a fortified area below.

In the Enclosure site at Ardnadam – No. 27 – the post holes and floors of two round houses were uncovered during excavation. These overlay the foundations of the Neolithic houses – Neolithic Gazetteer No. 9. The Iron Age houses were superimposed on each other i.e. the later one was probably a re-build of the earlier. The earlier one was 12m

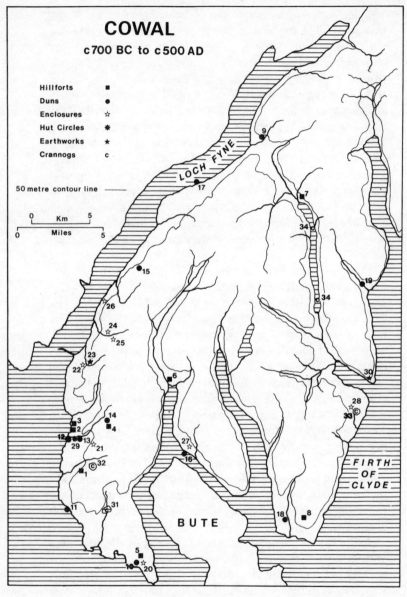

COWAL
c 700 BC to c 500 AD

Hillforts   ■
Duns   ●
Enclosures   ☆
Hut Circles   ✳
Earthworks   ★
Crannogs   c

50 metre contour line   ——————

0   Km   5
0   Miles   5

LOCH FYNE

FIRTH OF CLYDE

BUTE

4. Iron age sites

and the late 11.5m in diameter. Carbon taken from the later one was dated to the 1st century BC. The enclosing wall around the site at Ardnadam was discovered to have been built about the same period as the first house probably to contain it and as a protection against animals.

The dating and recognition of all of these sites is usually controversial and frequently impossible without excavation. Archaeological knowledge is ever increasing and one excavation can change the accepted facts completely. As has been proved at Ardnadam, Auchategan and at other areas, most settlement sites continue to be used for hundreds – if not thousands – of years. Before the nineteenth century a site that was good to live on in the Neolithic Period continued to be good, until the twentieth century when mankind insisted on having all modern conveniences.

Iron Age Sites

(An asterisk marks those sites which are worth a visit.)

Hillforts

1. **Auchalick Wood, Ardmarnoch**
   NR 920 740

This fort set within a heavily robbed single wall occupies nearly 2,000 sq.m. on the summit of a rocky knoll overlooking Auchlick Bay. The site is overgrown and the wall is now difficult to find as the animals no longer graze the ground. The entrance is to the west.

2. ***Barr an Taolain, Kilfinan**
   NR 920 813

In a clearing within a forestry plantation on a ridge above Loch Fyne, between Otter Ferry and Kilfinan there is an oval shaped fort. An area of about 900 sq.m. is enclosed on three sides by a stout wall built of massive blocks. The fourth side is naturally protected as it stands above a sheer cliff overlooking the sea. Access is by the forestry road.

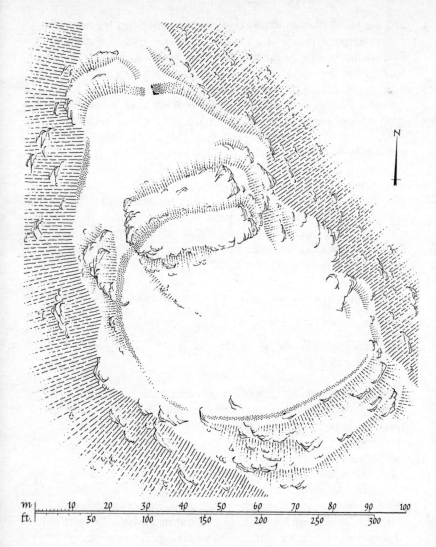

m	10	20	30	40	50	60	70	80	90	100
ft.		50	100	150	200	250	300			

Figure 2.   Barmore Fort

3. Barranlongairt, Otter Ferry
NR 921 815

This small fort lies about 250m north of Barr an Taolain on the other side of a small burn. It is very denuded but has been enclosed by a single stone wall which survives as a band of rubble. The entrance is probably to the south end. The area enclosed is about 800 sq.m.

4. Barr Lagan, Kilfinan
NR 941 822

Barr Lagan is an isolated rocky ridge 800m east of the B8000 and about equidistant from Otter Ferry and Kilfinan. The ridge is aligned N. to S. with the E. and W. sides rising steeply from the moorland. Reasonably easy access is available only at the north end. Little of the wall survives on each flank but on the N. and S. it appears as a low bank of stony rubble. The area enclosed is approximately 3,500 sq.m.

5. Caisteal na Sidhe, Ardlamont
NR 963 691

This fort is now heavily enclosed and smothered by forestry trees and its appearance and strength are difficult to appreciate. It is situated on a bluff above the Ardlamont road about 1km north of Kilbride Church and must have had an extensive view over the Ardlamont landscape and out to the sea approaches. It is enclosed by a massive dry stone wall which is still partly preserved. It has been suggested that, because of the spacing and direction of cavities which can be seen, the wall may have been timber-laced. i.e. It is suggested that it is a Timber-laced Fort which has not been fired and is therefore not vitrified. The area of the fort appears to be about 4,000 sq.m. but measurement is difficult.

6. *Barmore, Glendaruel
NS 002 823

Barmore is an isolated hill covering the entrance to Glendaruel. It stands above the A886 immediately S. of the junction with the Tighnabruaich road – the A8003. The fort is roughly circular enclosed by a tumbled stone wall. It has an annexe to the North through which the entrance track passes. Its area is about 2,500 sq.m.

7. *Invernoaden, Strachur
NS 121 976

The memorial to Harry Lauder's son at the N. end of Loch Eck is set on an isolated knoll which is the site of a probable stone-walled fort. The area enclosed is small – about 700 sq.m. – but the site is magnificent as it covers all the flat land at the head of Loch Eck.

8. Buchailean, Toward
NS 122 702

The flat-topped hill which dominates Toward was recorded as being fortified in the early records. However, there is now little evidence to support this. A stretch of built walling was noted at one side before the surrounding area was afforested and the animals were withdrawn from the land.

Duns

9. *An Dun, Inverglen, Strachur
NN 097 018

Immediately above a side road leading to Inverglen Farm from Strachur Clachan there is a tree-covered knoll. On the summit there are the remains of a dun and its outworks. The enclosing wall – 5m thick – surrounds an area 12m in diameter. Depressions within the tumbled wall may show the situation of former cells. An attached or underlying wall which encloses an area to the West of the Dun is recorded as an outwork although it may be the wall of an earlier Hillfort.

10. *Colachla, Millhouse
NR 954 683

350m S.W. of Colachla on the summit of a flat rocky ridge there is circular dun with extensive views across to Arran and the Ayrshire coastline. The walls are heather-covered and stand about 0.5m in height. Some of the inner and outer facing-stones can be seen, showing that the wall is approximately 3m thick. The entrance is on the N.N.E. The area enclosed is about 250m.

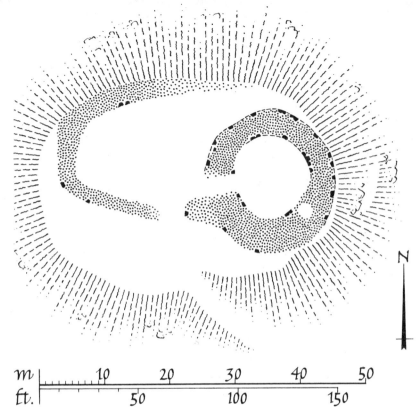

| m | | 10 | | 20 | | 30 | | 40 | | 50 |
| ft. | | | 50 | | | 100 | | | 150 | |

Figure 3. An Dun, Inverglen, Strachur

11. *Caisteal Aoidhe, Ardmarnoch
NR 909 710

A tidal island on the shore of Loch Fyne, 2km S. of
Ardmarnoch House is crowned with a heavily-vitrified dun
and its annexe. The vitrification is intense but on the N.E. arc
unburnt rubble still stands to a height of 3m above ground on
the outside. The walls appeared to have been about 3.5m
thick enclosing an area 11m in diameter. The annexe to the N.
is almost as big and the walls are impressive. The dun is most
easily reached from the private road through the estate. Just
before reaching Bagh Buic turn west into the hill and cross the
moorland in a westerly and then a south westerly direction for
about 500-600m.

40 COWAL

12. MacEwan's Castle, Kilfinan
NR 915 795

This rocky promontory extending into Loch Fyne and 2km
N.W. of Kilfinan has foundations on it belonging to the
Medieval period but they are enclosed by the stump of a stone
wall 3m broad. Excavations conducted there in 1968 and
1969 showed that the enclosing wall belonged to an earlier
Dun with a burnt entrance to the N. The area as about
400sq.m.

13. Barr Ganuisg, Kilfinan
NR 928 808

The slight remains of this Dun are on the sky line to the West
of the B8000 about 3km N. of Kilfinan. Afforestation now
masks it from the road although the Dun is not covered. Only
a section of walling about 5m thick remains.

14. *Barr Iola, Otter Ferry
NR 938 828

This is the best preserved Dun in the area with a magnificent
position. The wall of about 3m, though tumbled, still has the
inner and outer faces surviving for considerable stretches. The
entrance and a trackway leading to it can be traced on the W.
side. The area enclosed is about 400 sq.m. The rectilinear
foundation to the S. is probably of a relatively recent date.

15. Cnoc Creagach, Lephinchapel
NR 972 911

This Dun occupies the summit of a rocky knoll above the
birch wood N.N.E. of Lephinchapel Farm. Only a small
section of wall remains but it stands to a height of 1m, in six
rough courses. It occupies an area of about 200 sq.m.

16. Eilean Buidhe
NS 018 753

On the S.W. end of Eilean Buidhe, one of the Burnt Isles in
the Narrow of the Kyles of Bute, there is a vitrified Dun. It
was excavated in 1936 but is now heavily overgrown. The
Dun is circular, about 300 sq.m. within a wall some 4m broad.

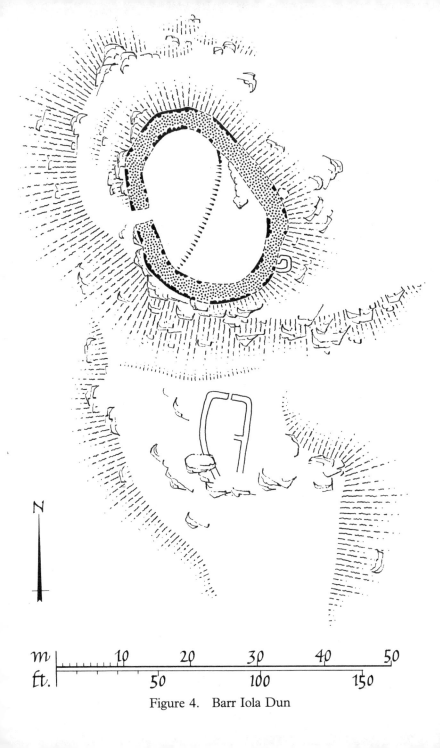

Figure 4.   Barr Iola Dun

17. *Eilean Math-ghamhna, Newton, Loch Fyne
NS 034 986

Across the bay from Newton an island lies off the end of the promontory. An oval-shaped Dun has been built on the flatter ground in the centre of the island. A band of rubble 4m broad encloses an area about 300 sq.m. A ruinous cross-wall to the S.E. may mark the position of outworks or an annexe.

18. *Dunan, Ardyne, Toward
NS 100 689

Clearly visible from Rothesay and from the farmlands around Ardyne Point there is a tree-covered knoll 45m high. It overlooks the construction yard on the shore to the S.W. A heavily robbed wall represented now by a low bank of rubble encloses an area of about 200 sq.m.

19. Dun Daraich, Glen Finart
NS 179 893

This is another vitrified Dun but it is so overgrown with rhododendrons that it is almost impossible to see. It is set on an isolated rocky knoll standing 15m above the floor of the glen. Only the vitrified stretches of wall and a few boulders along the edge remain, to show the size of the enclosure which was estimated to be about 200 sq.m. It lies on the N.E. side of the Glen Finart burn 500m N. of Barnacabber.

Enclosures

20. *Allt Thomais, Kilbride
NR 961 685

Amongst the trees, on the N. side of a small burn, within 50m of and on the W. side of the Ardlamont road opposite Colachla, there is a circular enclosure 12m in diameter. An enclosing stone wall 1.5m thick with inner and outer faces is visible in the undergrowth. There may have been two entrances with the flanking stones of a porch over the western one.

21. Dun Mor, Lindsaig, Kilfinan
NR 935 799

High above and to the north of Lindsaig Farm there is an

enclosure with an internal area of 500 sq.m. It has an extensive view over the Kilfinan valley and bay.

22. ⋆Tom Buidhe, Otter Ferry
NR 936 840

This site is almost opposite Kilail (NR 938 841) but on the S. side of the Kilail burn. It is set in the trees about 200m north of the sharp corner in the Otter Ferry/Glendaruel road. The corner is 200m S.E. of the hairpin junction with the B8000. The enclosure consists of about 500 sq.m. within a wasted wall measuring about 1.5m broad.

23. ⋆Kilail, Otter Ferry
NR 938 841

Set on a rocky isolated knoll about 200m above and to the N. of the Kilail burn and 1km from the shore there is an enclosure. Its walls are of stone about 3m in greatest thickness surrounding an area of about 30 sq.m. The site is clearly visible northwards from the Otter Ferry/Glendaruel hill road as it is under the power lines and marked by the poles.

24. ⋆Evanachan, Otter Ferry
NR 948 865

The slight remains of this enclosure are set on a natural terrace in a pasture field to the W. of the farmhouse. The farm and enclosure both stand at 25m O.D. above Loch Fyne. The enclosure is about 500 sq.m. within a bank 1m high.

25. ⋆Largiemore, Otter Ferry
NR 955 860

High on the moor above the chalets, and now surrounded by forestry plantation, there is a near-circular enclosure. It is about 20m in diameter with an entrance to the west through a low boulder-built wall 2.3m thick.

26. ⋆Lephinchapel, Loch Fyneside
NR 958 895

In the woods nearly 500m N. of Gortein, about 200m uphill from the road and 100m N. from the burn, there are two circular foundations. The stones forming them are deeply set in the ground and do not form continuous arcs. The upper one is slightly recessed into the hill so that the downslope side forms a lip and shows as a curved kerb. The enclosure measures 12m in diameter. The lower one, 14m in diameter, is about 100m to the west. No kerbing is visible but the stones of the enclosing wall are continuous for 300°.

27.   *Ardentraive, Colintraive
NS 025 755

This small enclosure overlooks the Narrows of the Kyles of Bute. It is situated on a level terrace immediately above the rock cutting where the old road joins the new Colintraive road – the A886. The enclosure is nearly circular 10m by 9m within a wall 2m thick with an entrance to the N.E.

28.   *Ardnadam, Dunoon
NS 163 791

To the west of the Dunoon/Sandbank road – A815 – at the point opposite the cemetery gates there is a gap in the trees on the hillside. In this gap is the Enclosure which was excavated over many years. The Enclosure is irregularly shaped and covers approximately 1 acre. The enclosing dyke has been ditched on the outside and consists of turf at one stretch and turf and stone at another. It stands about 0.75m high.

In the fourth level of the excavation the post holes of two round houses were uncovered, the one superimposed upon the other. It was considered that the first house had not been securely built and the second was a rebuilding of the first. The second was dated to the 1st century BC by carbon found in two of the post holes. The houses were 12m and 11.5m in diameter with an attached stone building which had outlasted both of the wooden structures (See Plan 12).

Hut Circles

29.   Barr Ganuisg, Kilfinan
NR 924 807

These are the only two genuine and accepted hut circles known in Cowal. They are now enclosed by forestry plantation and are safeguarded though very difficult to find in the undergrowth. They lie about 150m N.W. of the stone dyke which bounds the afforestation and 1km along the dyke from the B8000. The dyke meets the B8000 approximately 1.5km N. of Kilfinan. The circles are 6m in diameter and 6m by 5m and are within 60m of each other. Some excavation was made in the best preserved – the lower one – in the 1940s. Pottery was found but has since been lost.

Earthwork

30.   *Cnoc nam Fiantan, Strone
      NS 179 810
Situated on Strone Golf Course a slight platform can be seen on the skyline above the housing estate. Its appearance, tradition and a small excavation carried out a few years ago, showed that an enclosing turf bank set upon cobbles enclosed an area 30m in diameter. The 6th tee is set on the platform mound.

Crannogs

31.   Loch Asgog, Millhouse
      NR 947 704
When the level of Loch Asgog was lowered during the construction of the Powder Mills at Millhouse in the nineteenth century three crannogs became visible. It is said that local people robbed the piles which stood above the water.

32.   *Loch Meldalloch, Ardmarnoch
      NR 938 745
An island in this loch appears to have an underwater causeway reaching out to it. There is a modern rectangular building on the island and so any prehistoric foundations which may be there will be destroyed.

33.   Loch Loskin, Dunoon
      NS 169 788
It is thought that there is a crannog in the north end of the Loch.

34. Loch Eck
NS 140 874 & 141 946

Two islands in Loch Eck may be crannogs. The more southerly is now under water level and has never been inspected. The more northerly is called in Gaelic 'Cook's island'; further, the adjacent farm is named 'Island Farm' implying that the island had some importance. However, nothing of any significance can be seen on it.

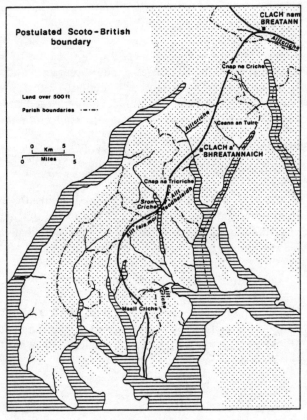

5. Drumalban

LATE IRON AGE
Roman Period. 43 AD to 410 AD

The dates of the Roman occupation of Britain do not apply to the north and west of Scotland (Alba). Even in the south of Scotland the Romans were in full control for only three short periods, each about twenty years between 79 AD and perhaps 220 AD. Nevertheless, throughout those 140 years and later, Roman sophistication must have influenced the Celtic tribes north and west of the Antonine Wall and almost dominated the tribes between the Walls. The knowledge that the Romans had slaughtered their forebears and now subjugated their kinsmen to the south and east must have been a constant irritant and an encouragement to the Northern tribes to raid and harry. Yet, for better or for worse, roads had been built where no roads had been, making communication easier and the infiltration of foreign ways unavoidable. Most Celts must have at least seen and handled Roman coins and the women must have coveted, if not treasured, a Samian dish, or Roman jewellery.

The geographer Ptolemy has given us the names and locations of some of the tribes who occupied North Britain in the 2nd century AD (Keppie '86). In the area we call Argyll, he places the Epidii in Kintyre, the Creones in Lochaber, and Dumnonii in the regions we recognise as Ayrshire, Renfrewshire and Dunbartonshire. W. J. Watson adds another possible tribal name to this list as he suggests that the Cerones who may be a branch of the Creones occupied mid-Argyll. The tribal names are written across Ptolemy's map and so it is impossible to tell the position of the tribal boundaries for which tribe owns the areas between the printed names. Cowal comes into this category as it lies between the land held by the Epidii, the Creones and the Dumnonii. It is a logical and well understood fact that in prehistoric and early historic times waterways did not divide territories, they united them. The lochs and rivers were the preferred routes for travelling rather than over the mountains and across bogs. Thus boundary lines stretched along the summit of the mountains and not along rivers and up the centre of lochs.

Such a boundary is postulated to have run through Cowal and to be a continuation of 'Druim Alban' – the ridge of Alba – which is the accepted boundary between the Dalriada and Pictland. This boundary is thought to be equivalent to the present boundary between Perthshire and Argyll. Its southern end is marked by a massive boulder on the hillside to the west of Glen Falloch – the 'Clach nam Breattan' – the boundary marker between the Scots, the Picts and the British of Strathclyde. (Kirby, '71) Another stone of similar dimensions and with a similar name – the Clach nam Brettanaich – stands on the hill above and to the N.W. of Lochgoilhead. Traditionally it is said to be the boundary marker between the Scots and the British. An imaginary line drawn across the crest of the hills between these two boulders suggests that Druim Alban continued south from Glen Falloch into and through Cowal.

The suggestion that this postulated boundary was genuine and continued south of Lochgoilhead is reinforced by the number of 'criche' and 'fola' names that mark its line. These are found on the top of the hills between the two stones and then southwards in a line that crosses Loch Eck and continues to Loch Striven near to Inverchaolain. The final name is 'Meall Criche' – the boundary hill – between Glen Lean and Loch Striven. (Plan 5). Both 'criche' and 'fola' are Gaelic words meaning 'a boundary'; 'fola' is an older term and is now obsolete. This line may have been the tribal border between the Dumnonii and the Cerones cutting the area we call Cowal and suggesting that the Dumnonii occupied the eastern and the Cerones the western parts. At that time 'Cowal' as an area would not exist.

Such a partition throughout prehistory is supported by the distribution maps of the different periods shown on plans 2, 3, and 4. The difference in numbers between the few sites to the east on the Clyde hinterland, compared with the large number on the west on Loch Fyne hinterland is significant. Further indicative evidence is known in the Iron Age although its illustration is beyond the range of plans 4 and 5. The entrance to the upper Firth of Clyde – from Portencross, to the Cumbraes and across to Bute – is covered by five known and one probable burnt timber-laced forts i.e. by five Vitrified forts. This suggests that the Firth may have been a closed waterway closed by, and under the control of, a particular tribe. That tribe was probably the Dumnonii who occupied the east side of the Firth. If so, all of the land around the Firth, including eastern Cowal, may have been managed and governed by them.

Plan 4 shows how thickly distributed the Iron Age sites are along Loch Fyneside. This compares well with the distribution across the Loch in Kintyre, Knapdale and Mid-Argyll and suggests a close relationship between the peoples on each side. Thus the land on both sides of Loch Fyne may have been under the control of the Cerones and the Epidii or at least to subordinate families associated with them. The name 'Epidii' is said to mean 'the tribe of the horse'. This may be a totem name or it may refer to the tribe's skill in rearing and trading horses. The family name McEachern is still known in Kintyre; it means 'the son of the horse lord'.

No evidence of Roman occupation nor even of a temporary Roman visit has yet been found in Cowal. In the early years viz. 81 AD. Agricola is recorded as having made at least one sea-crossing in the West and later despatched some ships up the west coast. No Roman marching camp nor its sea equivalent has been found but such a site may be waiting for someone with good observation. The only slight hint of the Roman presence was a mysterious road near Ardlamont Point which had Roman features and was discovered to be so old that peat had grown over it. Unfortunately its destination was lost under afforestation before it could be traced.

COWAL AT THE BEGINNING OF HISTORY

The Coming of Christianity – 500 AD

From about 300 AD onwards for three hundred years there
was a gradual settlement of peoples from the north-east coastline
of Erin (Ireland) to the western seaboard of Alba (Scotland).
The reason for the movement is not known but there may
have been a land hunger in Erin because of overpopulation and
land to spare in the territory of the Epidii and the Cerones in
the west of Alba. For whatever reason, by the late 6th century
a new kingdom, Dalriada – the kingdom of the 'Scottis' (the
raiders) was established in the territory we know as Argyll. Its
capital and one of its strongholds was the rock of Dunadd in
the great moss of Crinan just across Loch Fyne from Kilfinan
in W. Cowal. Dalriada's territory stretched northwards to the
area known today as Lochaber and eastwards over Loch Fyne.
For two hundred years Dalriada – the kingdom of the Scots –
waxed and waned as it came into conflict with Picts to the
north and the Britons to the east. Finally in 843 AD the
Scottish and Pictish Kingdoms were joined under the one
King – Kenneth McAlpine – and Scotland was born.

In the mid 5th century – about 432 AD – an escaped slave
returned to Erin to bring Christianity to his former masters. This
was St Patrick, the Patron Saint of Ireland. He was now an
ordained Bishop of the Christian church. It was a church whose
organization was based on the Roman civil service – each city
and surrounding countryside had its own dioceses with a governing bishop and priests serving under him. Already this
church had accumulated great wealth and probably rich vest-
ments and eucharistic vessels to match. When Patrick came to
preach and teach in Erin, he came to a country which had
never known Roman administration – there were no cities, no
roads, and no civil service. Each petty king was absolute ruler
in his own area. He would live in his own circular enclosure –
his rath – with his family, his warriors, and his servants around
him calculating his wealth in his cattle. Sometimes he would
raid the neighbouring rath to steal their cattle or perhaps to
take back his own which had been stolen previously.

Here also were the Druids – the custodians of the laws and traditions of the Celts – with their schools in which it would appear that some of their teaching must have been in sympathy with Christian precepts as no martyrdoms are known in Ireland. It is even thought that some of the Druidical schools were taken over by the earliest monastic schools and that possibly some of the trainee Druids after baptism became trainee monks. Little is known about the doctrines of the Druids except that they had a strong belief in life after death and as this was and is a precept of Christianity the Celts would accept it easily. It is also known that the Druids considered oak trees – or some of them – to be sacred and that they worshipped their gods in the open-air in clearings in the oak woods. This practice was accepted by the Christians and for many of the following centuries the Celtic peoples worshipped the Christian God in the open air.

Thus, the organisation and the outward manifestations of Roman Christianity changed to fit the way of life of the Celtic people. The key stone of administration was no longer a bishop but the monastic school. These were great enclosures where trainee 'missionaries' under an abbot gathered to learn the Faith and to copy the scriptures. Wandering monks or 'missionaries' then travelled far and wide from the schools with the book of the scriptures carried in a satchel on their back, sandals on their feet and a wooden staff in their hand. It is known that sometimes a 'king' when he had been converted to Christianity would give a rath – an enclosure – to a monk or to monks. This rath would then become the headquarters for a particular area, where the monks would live, and from where the Gospel would be preached and where the altar would stand on which the mass was celebrated. Here they, and eventually the Christians of the area, would be buried.

In 563 AD a high-born Christian monk called Columcille was in disgrace. His punishment was banishment to the new kingdom of Dalriada across the seas to the north. There he was charged with preaching the Christian faith to his kinsfolk who had emigrated from Erin and with winning souls for Christ. He founded a new monastic school on the island of Iona from where his monks travelled N.S. and E. teaching and preaching and in turn founding new monastic schools. The sites where the monks settled, even for short periods, became known as 'kils' – derived from 'cell'. The 'kil' became associated with the name of the founder monk or with the name of the monk's abbot or teacher and in time the doubly derived name became the geographic name of the place – Kilfinan, Kilmun, Kilmodan etc.

As in Ireland, it is possible that enclosures were given to the monks by the 'king' of the district but however the monks acquired them, the 'kil' sites usually were enclosed by a turf or stone dyke and frequently they were round – like the Irish raths. For centuries there would be no stone building in them. The monks' sleeping and eating places would be built of timber; the altar would be a slab of stone set up in the open air and the preaching place would be a mound where the monk could be seen and heard. Eventually, the altar might be set within a small wooden building – a chapel – but the chapels were so small that only the monk celebrating the Mass would be inside. By about 900 AD chapels were being built – or partly built – in stone. After another 200 years or so the Celtic forms of worship were finally abandoned and larger chapels into which the congregation could enter were built. Frequently these churches were built on top of, or at least within the same enclosures, as the earlier wooden buildings. Thus it is that today some Parish Churches are built within a round or near-round enclosure.

Cowal and Kintyre (Plan 5) have a greater percentage of place names with the prefix 'kil' than anywhere else in the country which indicates the direction of the movement of the wandering monks from Ireland. Not all of these preaching sites can be traced on the ground and many have been lost by being built over or ploughed out. Of the old enclosures which can be found – a very few have the foundation of the early stone chapel within them (13 & 24); others have the foundation of a medieval church within (9 & 19), and still others enclose the church that is in use today (1). The sites which are known with their enclosed foundations or structures are listed in the gazetteer.

There is another group of sites which have recently been

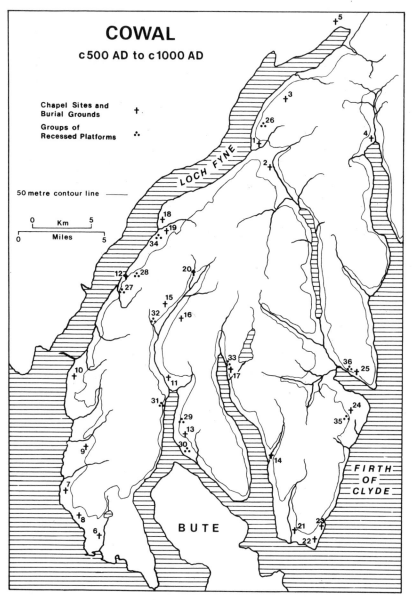

6. Early Christian sites

recognised and which seem to belong to this period i.e. the period known in Scotland as Early Christian – 500 AD to 1,000 AD. These sites are groups of Recessed Platforms. The Platforms are round flat areas which have been levelled by cutting back into the slope of a hillside and by throwing forward the excavated soil to form a built front lip. The platforms in any one group may range from 6m diameter to 10m diameter and from sea level to 200m altitude. A few single Platforms are known but they usually occur in groups of any number from 2 to 70. Six have been excavated in Cowal and five of these were built as the foundation for round timber-framed structures. The sixth was indeterminate. Two of the timber buildings were classed as houses as hearths were found on the floor. A range of dates calculated from carbon taken from floors or post holes gives a span of time from 3rd century to 13th century AD. The Platform groups are listed in the gazetteer.

Although these sites are named 'Charcoal-burning Stances' in Vol. 7 of the Inventory of the R.C.A. & H.M.S. evidence given by survey work and excavation both in Cowal and elsewhere in the West, suggests that these groups of Platforms are settlement sites (hillside villages). Some of them have been reused for charcoal burning. It is considered that the Platforms are foundations for timber buildings, and that these buildings are representatives of all of the structures that are usually found in a farm complex today. Thus, as well as dwelling-houses there will be byres, worksheds, haylofts, hen houses and pig stys etc. It is very possible that some of the structures have been built on level ground. If so, they cannot be identified as nothing would remain of a wooden structure above the turf. It is only on sloping ground that the necessary round foundation platform indicates a hut site.

Distribution maps both for Cowal and other western areas show that there may be an association between the groups of Platforms and the Early Christian sites. The association may be illusory but as the carbon dates cover the Early Christian Period such a relationship is logical. The proposition is that some of the Platforms may belong to the late Iron Age Period and that these parts of the settlements may have been in existence when the Christian mission began from Ireland. The monks would then settle near to where people were living, to influence them and teach them. Throughout the 7th to the 11th centuries the settlements would grow and the Christian site would become the regular place of worship for the area. Eventually by the 12th century the form of worship changed and the Christian sites were either deserted or developed and the hillside Platforms abandoned. It is suggested that at that time the building of rectangular houses may have begun and that the post holes or floors of these may underlie the 18th and 19th century townships which are known to us today as deserted townships.

The Viking raids and eventual settlement of the Norsemen also belong to this period – the first millennium of the Christian Era. For 200 years from about the mid-8th century the monastic communities and probably the secular communities too, lived in fear of being pillaged, raped, made homeless and eventually slaughtered by the Vikings. However, the Norsemen like the Scottis 500 years earlier settled and intermarried and in 1,000 AD adopted Christianity.

Only in Orkney and Shetland are many Norse settlements recognised. On the islands and western seaboard of Argyll it is probable that many of their houses underlie the long houses of the late Gaels. In Cowal, sheltered from the Western Seaways, there may have been little settlement. However, the deserted townships which are on the coasts open to the lower Firth of Clyde and Loch Fyne may have originated in Viking times. Two house foundations on the south end of Bute are thought to be Norse and on that island also a Viking 'hog-backed' tombstone was found.

In Cowal there are a few place names which suggest Norse influence. There are the deserted townships of Coustonn and Troustan on Loch Striven side – nos. 55 and 56 on Plan 10 – also Laglingartan – no. 57 on the N.E. side of Loch Fyne, and Ornidale, Loch Riddon.

EARLY CHRISTIAN SITES (PROBABLE)

Chapel sites and Burial grounds

In the later Medieval Period a church was built on some of these sites. Those sites which continued in use are identified by 'M.P' and the index number of the entry in the gazetteer of the Medieval Period.

Sites worth visiting are marked with an asterisk.

1. ***Kilmolash, Strachur**
   NN 095 015

Strachur church yard is typical of an Early Christian Site which has been used for, perhaps, over 1000 years The yard is circular and mounded suggesting graves and early foundations under the turf (M.P. 1).

2. **Chapelverna, Strachur**
   NN 100 005

No remains of this chapel can now be found. It was thought to be medieval but as the dedication was to St. Marnoch, there may have been an early foundation (M.P. 2).

3. ***St. Catherine's, Loch Fyne**
   NN 125 073

This is a medieval foundation but it is entered here as there may have been as earlier structure (M.P.3).

4. ***Church of the Three Holy Brethren, Lochgoilhead**
   NN 198 014

There is a record of a foundation on this ground in the 7th century and though the name suggests early origins, no one knows the identity of the three Holy Brethren. The site is on a through E.–W. route (M.P. 6).

5. ***Kilmorich, head of Loch Fyne**
   NN 189 128

300m W. of the Inveraray/Arrochar road (A83) immediately N. of the Oyster Bar, there is an old burial ground. The evidence of a chapel, if there ever was one within the enclosure, has disappeared. A cross marked on the O.S. map 1.5 km above and to the W. is now resting against the wall of the modern Kilmorich church at Cairndow. Originally the cross may have marked the route across the hills to Kilmorich (M.P. 5).

6. *Stillaig, Millhouse
NR 938 686

A visible rectangular turf foundation within an enclosure is to be seen on the moor W. of the Stillaig Bay private road. The foundation is traditionally said to be a chapel but nothing is known about it.

7. Ardmarnoch, Loch Fyne
NR 912 727

There were the foundations of a chapel here until the end of the 18th century. The field is known as St. Marnoch's field.

8. Cnoc na Cille, Glennan, Loch Fyne
NR 925 705

The rectangular stone foundations of a building lying E.–W. stands within an enclosure on a natural terrace of a small hill above Glennan Bay. In the east end of the building there is a large slab of stone which suggests an altar. Local tradition claims there is an ancient Christian burial ground on the hillslope – hence the name 'Cnoc na Cille'. The rectangular foundations may therefore be a chapel.

9. *Kilfinan, Loch Fyne
NR 934 788

The appearance and name of this site suggests that this is an Early Christian site. The graveyard is mounded, and was circular although it does not now appear to be so, as in the early 19th century the road was re-routed through the yard. (M.P. 7).

10. Kilail, Otter Ferry
NR 934 843

The only evidence that such a chapel existed is the name of a field on the farm – 'Dail a Chaibeil' (Chapel Field). Stones which were believed to be the foundation of the chapel were

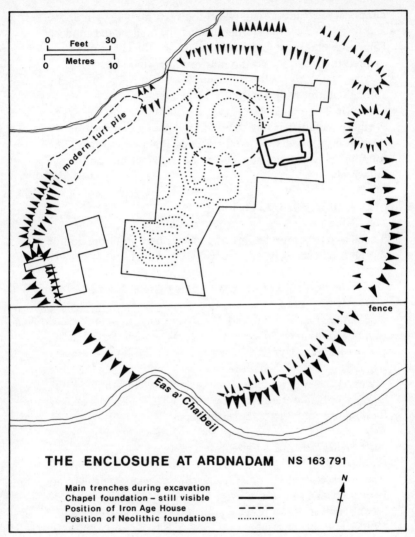

0 Feet 30
0 Metres 10

modern turf pile

fence

Eas a' Chaibeil

THE ENCLOSURE AT ARDNADAM NS 163 791

N

Main trenches during excavation
Chapel foundation – still visible
Position of Iron Age House
Position of Neolithic foundations

7. Ard na Dam Enclosure

found 200 m S. of the farmhouse close to the river.

11. *Kilmodan, Glendaruel
NR 995 841

The foundation of this site is traditionally in the Early
Christian period. The early site was said to be on the hillside
above and to the N.E. of the present building. The foundation
of a small building which is on a terrace at NS 000843 may be
the remains of that early chapel. Its walls were uncovered the
same time as the excavation of the adjacent Neolithic site
(Marshall, 1977). The present church is described in the
Medieval Gazetteer (M.P.8).

12. *Lephinchapel, Lochfyneside
NR 966 906

The tumbled and grass-covered foundations of this chapel are
in a rectangular enclosing dyke close to the loch 300m W. of
Lephinchapel Farm. Little is known about the site.

13. *Fearnoch, Colintraive
NS 021 764

No record or even tradition remains of this small ruined building. Nevertheless, its appearance, dimensions and associated
features proclaim it to be one of the few remaining stone Early
Christian Chapels. It is within a small enclosure; its breadth to
length is as 2:3; it lies approximately E.–W.; within 50m there
is a spring, traditionally said to be a 'tobar-a-bhaistidh' – a
Well of Baptism. The site is in a sheltered and hidden dell
surrounded by hills which themselves were surrounded by oak
woods – a classic description of a Columban site. It can be
reached from the road bridge over the burn on the A688.
Climb the hill to the N.W. for about 500m.

14. St Bride's, Inverchaolain
NS 093 755

The earlier site of Inverchaolain Church can still be traced as
a low mound in the grass above the road way into Stronyaraig
Farm. The dedication to Bride suggests that the site is
medieval but this is uncertain. (M.P. 11).

Figure 5.
Feornoch Chapel

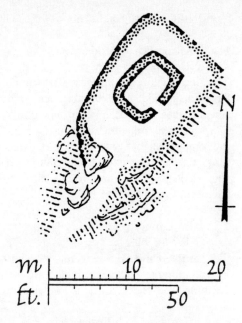

Figure 6.
Kildalven Burial Ground,
Chapel

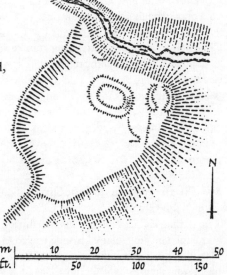

15. Kildalven, Glendaruel
NS 018 891

This site marked 'Burial Ground' on the O.S. map stands at 150m above the floor of Glendaruel. It is enclosed by earthen dykes. Faint mounding within the enclosure may show the foundations of a chapel. There is a deep circular depression set into the enclosing turf dyke which could be a cell or may only be a lime kiln.

16. Kilnaish (Gill an Nathois), Glendaruel
NS 021 876

A forestry plantation now obscures this site. Tradition asserts it was a place of burial and a monk's cell stood on the spot.

17. *Ardtaraig, Loch Striven
NS 056 826

The foundations of a building are in the grass beside the driveway 200 m W. of the house. There are no known traditions about the site except that it was a chapel. An upright stone with a pecked cross cut into it stands about 20m to the W of the foundation and reinforces the theory.

18. *Kilbride, Strathlachlan
NS 007 966

This is a particularly interesting site. Nothing however is known of its origins. It is found on the Strathlachlan peninsula 2km W. of the road – the B8000. It is best approached by a track leading 1.5 km to the N. of Castle Lachlan. The site consists of an enclosing circular dyke, 1.3m high and 2.6m thick within which are the foundations of a chapel. The surrounding dyke or 'cashel' suggest that a rath may have been adapted to ecclesiastical use but whether in Early Christian times or later could only be discovered by excavation. There is a well – Tobar an Longairt – 450m to the east. The foundations around the 'cashel', belong to a township of the 18th and 19th centuries. The township would be associated with Portindrain – No. 18 – in the Deserted Settlement gazetteer.

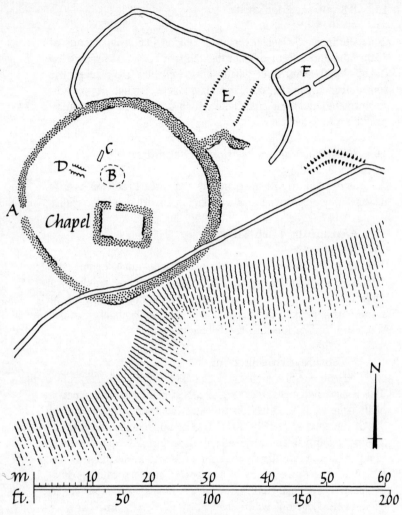

Figure 7.   Chapel of Kilbride, Chapel; Enclosure

19.   *Kilmorie, Strathlachlan
NS 010 951

The Kilmorie churchyard which is still in use is nearly circular and encloses the ruins of a medieval church. The shape of the burial ground and the dedication to St Maelrubha imply strongly that the site is an Early Christian foundation. The fact that Kilbride, NS 007 966 (No. 18) is only 1.75km to the N. makes the early dating of one of them suspect and Kilmorie has the best claim. Nevertheless they are on different sides of the river and each might have served differing communities even in Early Christian times.

The Kilmorie site is by the N. side of the B8000 between the caravan site and Inver restaurant (M.P. 9).

20. Kilbride, Glendaruel
NS 028 903

Information was given by the landowner that the site of the chapel of St Bride was destroyed many years ago. It was in the area now occupied by a quarry on the side of the Glendaruel west road.

21.   *Killenane/Killellan, Toward
NS 107 689

In a field known as the 'Chapel field' 500m S. of Kilellan farm and 300m W. of the road – the A815 – there is an ancient burial ground. Part of an enclosure can be traced beside, and is damaged by, a field track. Within the N. end of the enclosure there are traces of a possible foundation which might be a chapel.

22.   St. Mary's, Toward
NS 116 682

There is a tradition of a chapel and burial ground under the lawn of Tollard House. The dedication implies that the foundation is late.

23.   Chapelhall, Innellan
NS 139 689

The foundations of a chapel here, beside the Toward road,

were said to be 'distinctly visible' in 1864. A long cist containing a skeleton was uncovered some years ago and another three long cist burials are known to have been found.

24. *Ardnadam, Dunoon
NS 163 791

The tradition that the enclosure here was an ancient burial ground and that there had been within it a chapel, initiated the excavation of the site. (See the Neolithic and the Iron Age chapters.) The chapel with its altar base was uncovered in the early years of the excavation but although the post holes of an early wooden chapel were sought they were not discovered. However, other features were found which predated the chapel but were in the Early Christian levels and overlay the Iron Age Round Houses. These features were a probable outdoor altar, a preaching stance, an enclosure, a probable 'cell', graves and marker stones from the graves. (Plan 12)

The indications were very strong that the large enclosure which dated from the last centuries BC had been bequeathed to, or at least had been taken over by, Christian monks and used as their centre. Its translation to a Christian site was probably in the middle of the first millennium AD and its abandonment, around the 12th century. Three cross-marked stones found on the site are now in the Huntarian Museum in Glasgow. It is possible that this site is the forerunner of the medieval site at Kilmun. Whether or not they were contemporary or in succession, there must have been constant movement between the two places at the later period for the ferry crossing the Holy Loch from Kilmun to the S. side of the loch was linked to the Ardnadam site by a direct track.

25. *Kilmun, Holy Loch
NS 166 820

Tradition states that St Fintan Munnu of Tech Munno in Ireland was the founder of this Christian site but as stated above, the tradition may relate to the Ardnadam site (M.P.12).

Groups of Recessed Platforms
(N.G.R. applies to central areas)

26. Creggans, Strachur
NN 095 040

These Platforms are cut into the hill above and on the E. side
of the straight road north of the Creggans Hotel. They extend
along the hillside for nearly 2kms and up the hill to the 200m
contour. The area covered is about 100 acres but most of it is
now afforested. 60 platforms were found; the majority being
6, 7, and 8m although six were of 9m.

27. *Lephinchapel (South), Lochfyneside
NR 960 895

Lephinchapel Farm and the chapel site, lie between two
Groups of Platforms which are distinguished by 'North' and
'South'. The south Group is the larger and covers about 140
acres of hillside lying between the shore and 150m altitude. In
that area there are 82 known Platforms; two are big ones of
9m and 10m but the majority are 7m and 8m in diameter. One
of these was completely excavated and the ground plan of a
round timber-framed house was uncovered. No dating
material was found but it was shown that it pre-dated the 18th
century by a long period as the surface of the Platform had
been re-used probably in the mid-19th century by charcoal
makers working for the Iron Furnace across the loch at
Furnace. When first built the front lip of the platform had
been constructed in stone but by the time the charcoal burners
were working the stone work had completely collapsed.

The two round enclosures described in the Iron Age
gazetteer under NR 958 895 are both set on natural terraces
immediately below some of the Platforms.

28. *Lephinchapel (North), Lochfyneside
NR 970 910

Some of these Platforms are built in extraordinary positions
above and on the edge of broken rock cliffs. From there they
stretch eastwards on to the moors for nearly 1 km to about the
150m contour. 58 are known and they cover 72 acres of the

hillside. 22 of them are of 7m, 16 of 8m, 5 of 9m and the rest smaller. The small Dun – Cnoc Creagach, NR 972 911 – is immediately above and to the east of some of the Platforms

29.   Feorline, Loch Riddon
NS 014 785

The Feorline Group is a small one of nineteen Platforms set in about 41 acres. The new Colintraive road – the A886 – cuts the group though the majority of the platforms lie above and to the east. Although most of the group lie to the west of the Forestry plantation, the bracken has now invaded the ground and even in winter the platforms are masked by a mattress of dead bracken.

30.   *Ardentraive, Colintraive
NS 025 758

The site of this Group lies on the east side of the A886 about 1km N.W. of the ferry terminal at Colintraive. Here there are forty-four platforms on about 115 acres of hillside. The majority are 7 and 8m in diameter though there are a few bigger and smaller ones. One was fully excavated and it was found to be the foundation of a round timber-framed house which had been burned down. The date of the house was about 1000 AD. The enclosure at NS 035 755 described in the Iron Age gazetteer, was on a terrace below but surrounded by the Platforms.

31.   *Lochhead, Loch Riddon
NS 003 825

This is a very small group of fourteen platforms covering only 25 acres. They can be found in the woods on the W. side of Loch Riddon above the stretch of old road before the new section of road leaves the shore and starts to climb up to the viewpoint.

32.   Achanelid, Glendaruel
NS 013 882

Three small groups of platforms have been found in Glendaruel. There may be more groups and/or the known Groups

Standing Stones, Stillaig.

Ach Na Ha Chambered Cairn.

Caisteal Aoidhe.

Fearnoch Chapel, Glendaruel with enclosure wall.

Kilbride Chapel, Strathlachlan.

Asgog Castle.

Carrick Castle.

Church of the Three Holy Brethren, Lochgoilhead.

Grave slab, Kilmodan.

Kilmodan Church, Glendaruel.

Kilmodan Church, Glendaruel.

Taunich township.

Butter Bridge.

Otter Ferry slip-pier.

Clachaig powder mill. Double-walled magazine.

might be larger. So much is under forestry plantation that it is not possible to search. The group that is indexed is away from the coniferous trees and so it is thought to be complete. It is partly in oak scrub and partly on the moor, above the west road just to the north of Achanelid farm. Twelve platforms have been found on 15 acres of hillside.

33.   *Ardtaraig, Loch Striven
   NS 057 835
The main road – the B836 – cuts through this Group as it slopes steeply down to the side of the Loch from Glen Lean. Twenty-five platforms have been found on about 75 acres of steep hillside. Thirteen of them are 7m in diameter the others are bigger and smaller.

34.   Barnacarry, Strathlachlan
   NS 005 946
This is a small group set on an extremely steep hill and now completely enclosed in a forestry plantation. It is across the road and a little S.W. of the Inver restaurant. Fourteen Platforms have been recognised on about 26 acres. Eight of them are 7m in diameter.

35.   Ardnadam/Dunloskin, Dunoon
   NS 165 791
On the two hillsides surrounding and above the enclosure at Ardnadam (see ref. above) there is a group of forty platforms spread over an area of about 85 acres and extending up hill to the 100m contour. Those to the S. of the burn are mostly 9m in diameter; those to the N. are smaller – 7m diameter.

Three have been excavated or partially excavated. The fully excavated platform was the site of the occupation described in the Neolithic gazetteer under the reference NS 163 789. The original platform had been cut as a foundation for the Neolithic Round house. On top of its floor, after a long period of abandonment another round timber frame structure had been built; finally after another period of abandonment in the 13th/14th century AD the surface overlying the round hut floor was used as a working area. Shreds of pottery of these

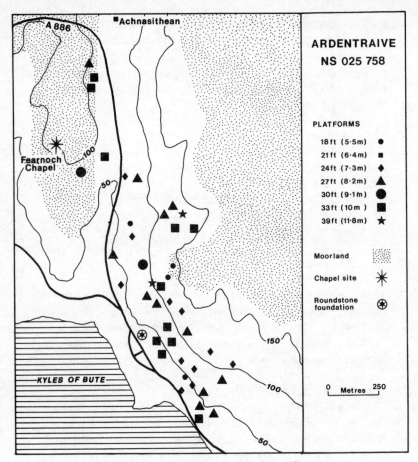

Figure 8   Ardentraive Platform Group

dates were taken from the floor along with iron slag.

Each of the two which were partially excavated – both on the N. side of the burn – showed evidence that the Platforms had been built to support round timber structures. The evidence was of post holes through the floors and through the front lips.

36. Kilmun, Holy Loch
NS 161 832

There were only eight platforms here and only one remains at all visible, as the others were so badly damaged by forestry cutting in the late 1960s that they are virtually destroyed. Nevertheless, they are recorded here as they may have had some association with the Kilmun Church site below. The platforms were set in a line apparently along an old road whose line was enclosed and re-used as a track by the forestry workers who laid out the Arboretum. The road seemed to go towards the church site at Kilmun. The platforms were alongside the track where it has climbed to nearly 250m. Thereafter the N. end of the track is lost in undergrowth.

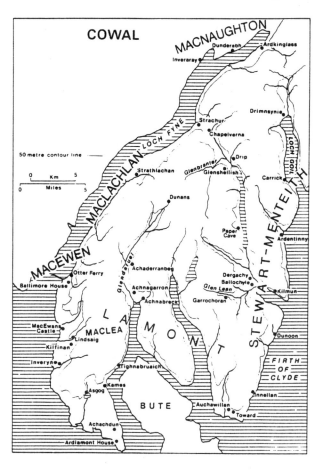

COWAL FAMILIES FROM THE 12TH TO THE
18TH CENTURIES

As was stated in the section 'The Coming of Christianity'
there was a gradual settlement and a constant coming and
going of peoples from Erin to Alba from about the 300 AD
onwards. By 500 AD a royal family was ruling the territory of
Dalriada in Alba and in the last quarter of the century a prince
of that Royal House – Aedan – was consecrated by Columba
as the first Christian king. Earlier in the century it is said that
a forbear of Aedan's – Comgall – had been the ruler. He or his
descendants may have had a special interest in eastern
Dalriada for that area still bears his name – Comhghall or
Cowal. It is debatable if the eastern side of Cowal, the area
bordering the Firth of Clyde, was part of this territory. The
partition which was postulated as existing in the Roman
period may have existed up to the 10th and 11th centuries.
(Plan 5). However it is accepted that Cowal was part of the
kingdom of Dalriada and did include both sides of Loch Fyne
as far south as Minard on the west side.

Although the new colony of Dalriada had its own king and
establishment, until the early 600s it was still under the
authority of the O'Neills, the High Kings of Erin. Thereafter
it claimed its independence and became one of the embryo
kingdoms of the future Scotland along with Pictland,
Strathclyde and Northumbria. The inhabitants of Cowal at
this time and later would be the progeny of the indigenous
Celtic tribes and the incoming Scottis from Ulster. Even after
the Dalriadic Kingdom of Alba had thrown off the governing
yoke of Ulster it is known that there was still a constant
movement of families between Erin and Alba and inter
marriages between the royal families of both countries. It is
documented that in the 11th century a prince of the house of
O'Neill – Aedh Anradhan – married a princess of Dalriada
and from this many of West Highland families claim their
descent. In Cowal the families of the Lamonts, the
Maclachlans, the MacLeas and the MacEwans; and across
Loch Fyne the MacNeills, the MacGilchrists, the MacSorleys

and the MacSweens may all stem from this union. In early Medieval times they must have been all-powerful on the Western seaboard, and were so enterprising that they built the first stone castle in Scotland – Castle Sween in Knapdale.

It is not known how soon these family names were recognised. Although the families may have been occupying the land before the 12th century, it was not until the 13th before the names 'Lagman' (Lamont), and 'Lachlan' were documented and the 14th before 'Ewan' was noted.

In the 12th century the territorial extent of the Irish families to the East of Cowal – particularly the Lamonts – is unknown. East Cowal might have been under the same ownership as the sherriffdom of Renfrew i.e. the High Stewards. Certainly by the mid-13th century lands in East Cowal and far West of Cowal are claimed by the Stewart/Menteiths though an earlier ownership is not documented.

LAMONT It is said that the Lamonts were the original kindred of Comgall. In 1200 Ferchar was chief and a generation later his sons granted the lands of Kilfinan to the monks of Paisley Abbey. Ferchar's grandson Ladman was the progenitor from whom the Clan Lamont derives its name. His son – Ferchar's great grand son – was known as 'Mac Laomain mor Chomhail uile' – 'Great Ladman's son of all Cowal;'. Whether or not this implied that the land bordering the Clyde was part of Cowal is uncertain. There is doubt about who, in the 11th century built Dunoon Castle and owned the surrounding land. Later the Lamont Chief was known as Lamont of Iveryne suggesting that Inveryne – not Dunoon – between Tighnabruaich and Kilfinan, was their earliest seat. Ascog and Toward the two castles associated with them in historical times are described in chapter 8. After the massacre and destruction of Toward Castle the Lamont chiefs lived in Ardlamont House until it was sold in 1893. Many Lamonts changed their name to Black after the massacre.

MACLACHLAN The Maclachlans also claim direct descent from the O'Neill kings of Ireland. The clan takes its name from Lachlan Mór who lived in the mid-13th century. At that time Lachlan owned as much land on the west side of Loch Fyne as they now do on the east side. The Maclachlans supported Bruce in the Wars of Independence and in the following centuries married into the clan who rose to supremacy in Argyll – the Campbells – and thus retained their lands and castle. In the '45 uprising Lachlan Maclachlan – the 17th Chief – raised his clan for Prince Charles and was killed at Culloden. Castle Lachlan was then bombarded from the sea into a ruin. In the new Castle Lachlan which was then built, Marjorie Maclachlan of Maclachlan, – the 24th Chief, lives today.

MACEWAN The Clan Ewan also traces its descent from Anradan. Their earliest historical forbear was a Ewan of Otter who flourished on the shores of Loch Fyne about 1200. The MacEwans may still have been in possession of the land in 1447 as a charter was witnessed by a MacEwan of Otter at that date. Thereafter Clan Ewan seems to have been without a Chief, a homeland or archives. The Barony of Otter consisted of lands both on the north and south of the spit at Otter. Traditions states that some MacEwans are buried on the Motte at Ballimore House. A fortification on a rock point on the north of Kilfinan Bay is called 'MacEwan's Castle'. However partial excavation of the site in 1970 showed that an early occupation belonged to a period long before the 11th century and a later occupation, to the 16th century.

MACLEA The Macleas may or may not be one of the original clans of Cowal. They were associated with the Lamonts as surgeons and notaries and held the lands of Lindsaig through them. As tradition states that they also were of Irish descent and held Lindsaig for 700 years the implication is that they are original and were in Cowal for as long as the Lamonts. However, another tradition connects them to the island of Lismore where Macleays were the keepers of the staff of St Moluag. It may be that the two traditions relate to two different families. Nevertheless, as both are said to have changed their name to Livingstone in the 17th century the implication is that they are one and the same.

MACNAUGHTON They came first to the Dubh Loch in Glen Shira near Inveraray, and later to Dunderave (See No. 6 of the Castle Gazetter). Both moves were at the instance of the Earl of Argyll. It is said that their castle by the Dubh Loch was abandoned in the late 15th century when plague ravished it.

STEWART and MENTEITH Walter Stewart, third son of the High Steward of Scotland married Mary Countess of Menteith in the mid 13th century and thereby he and his descendants inherited that Earldom. Their second son, Sir John Menteith, perhaps unjustly vilified as the betrayer of Wallace, seems to have had lands in Knapdale and Kintyre by 1262. It seems likely that this was part of a steady Stewart expansion westward into Cowal and Bute, from their base in Renfrewshire. The Stewart acquisition of lands around Kilmun and Loch Goil at a time which is not known, is probably part of this process. When exactly they acquired Dunoon Castle is also unclear; it may well predate their elevation to the throne under Robert II in 1372 when Dunoon became a Royal castle.

In 1296 a Stewart/Menteith signed himself as 'de Denune' on the Ragman Roll. This was the register of all of the Scots who swore fealty to Edward I before the Wars of Independence. It may be that the Stewart/Menteith 'de Denune' was given the lands of Dunoon at that time. It may be that a traditional and long-accepted ownership was at that time given Edward's royal assent, as it is possible that the rock of Dunoon and the surrounding land had always been under the same control as the land on the East of the River Clyde. What is sure is that by the 14th century the Stewart Kings owned Dunoon Castle.

CAMPBELL The Campbells were originally Britons of Strathclyde who came into Argyll through a marriage to the heiress of the O'Duines of Loch Awe. Their rise to unequalled power in the Highlands was due to their support of Robert the Bruce; thereafter they were ever increasingly used by the Crown as the means of subduing and controlling the Lords of the Isles and their successors.

Their rewards were great and they spread over much of Cowal. The main families included the Campbells of Strachur descended from the early 13th century Duncan Duf and probably senior by birth to the eventual Chiefs of the Loch Awe line. The exact date of their acquisition of Strachur is unknown but they were there by the middle of the 14th century with further grants of land in Glen Croe and on Loch Long. A branch of the MacIvor Campbells held Ballochyle near Dunoon. On Loch Fyne, the Campbells of Otter descend from the bloodthirsty George Campbell of Kinnochtrie, Sheriff Clerk of Argyll in the Civil Wars. The Campbells of Auchinbreck ('11' of Castle Gazetter) took their designation from the lands at the foot of Glendaruel. Their main land holdings, however, were on the other side of Loch Fyne. The main Campbell family in Cowal were the Campbells of Ardkinglas ('7' of Castle Gazetter) at the head of Loch Fyne, and their cadets who included the Campbell lairds of Auchawillan, Innellan ('14' – Castles) Dergachy, Drimsynie, Ardentinny and the families who provided the Captains of both Dunoon ('15' – Castles), and Carrick ('16' – Castles) as Keepers – the Earls, and later, the Dukes of Argyll.

The mountains on the N.W. side of Loch Eck were hunting grounds of the Campbells. In a cave on this hillside family documents of the Argyll family were hidden for safe keeping in the stormy times of the late 17th century. The cave is formed by a rock fall – a massive part of the hillside has slipped downwards allowing the crest of the fallen mass to lean against the rock face thus forming a dry shelter. The 'Paper Cave' is now in afforestation which has recently been replanted after felling. It can be reached from a forestry road but the ground is rough and steep. The N.G.R. is NS 137 894.

Other families

Cowal has been the location of a number of smaller families of no great power but in several cases of baronial rank and of ancient origin.

Among them are the FERGUSONs or MACKERRIS, latterly of Glen Shellich. They are the chieftains of Clannfhearguis of Strachur and claim to be the oldest clan in Scotland. It is not impossible that they were of Dalriadic Royal descent. They were probably the earliest owners of the Strachur area and when the Campbells took over, they became their Officers or the Stewards of Strachur.

The MACOLCHYNYCHEs, some of whom later took the name MACKENZIE held Chapelverna ('2' – E.C. gazetteer) 'past all memory of man' well into the 19th century.

The FLETCHERs moved to Dunans in 1745 in upper Glendaruel having been displaced by the Campbells from Achalader at the head of Glenorchy where as fletchers or arrowmakers to the MacGregor chiefs they had been the original inhabitants.

The MACANANICHs or BUCHANANs as they later styled themselves, of Achaderranbeg were said to descend from the tax-collector left behind on their lands in Cowal by the early Campbell chiefs.

The servants of St Munn – whence came Kilmun – were the MACILMUNs of MACPHUNs who held Inneraodan and Drip. The story of MacPhun of Drip's miraculous recovery in the 17th century after having been hanged is well known. His body was delivered to his wife at Inveraray but in the boat crossing to Strachur he was revived and lived for a considerable numbers of years thereafter.

The Barons MACGIBBON were proprietors of Achnagarron and appear to have held their land directly from the king although they were among the late arrivals to the district.

A family of CURRIEs or MACVURICHs had held Ballilone in Bute from the 16th century and Garrachoran in Glen Lean from the 18th century, though both are now lost to them. Their representative's claim to the Chief of the family, who held the important position of Sennachies to the Lords of the Isles, has yet to be made good.

The MACBRAYNEs of Glenbranter have the arms of O'BRIEN but a more likely origin may be a legal one as MacBrehon or 'son of the judge'. Although said to belong to Argyllshire they are 'modern' arrivals in Cowal.

CASTLES AND MOTTES

From the 12th century to the 16th century

Donjons, and towers, and castles grey
Stand guardian by the winding way.

Generally the Mottes belong to the 12th century. They are monuments to the period when the Throne through the Anglo-Norman lords was attempting to subdue and control the ancient West Highland families. The mottes throughout the country were earthen mounds surrounded by a ditch, which were hurriedly thrown up, and on which a wooden structure was built.

The mound on which the remains of Dunoon Castle stand, appears to be a 'scarped motte', i.e. a natural hill whose sides were scraped to make it defensible. There may have been a wooden structure on it before the stone castle was built. As is stated in the 'FAMILIES' chapter, this scarped motte may have been the work of the Stewarts but nothing is documented. The other mottes described may be associated with the western movement of the Stewart/Menteiths.

With the exception of Old Castle Lachlan all the Cowal castles of which there are extant remains, fall into the general group of tower houses of which there are or were many hundreds in Scotland. The reasons for their popularity were that they were cheap to build of readily acquired materials, they required no special skills in building and they were sufficiently strong to be able to resist any force likely to attack them. They could not, of course, withstand cannon as was amply demonstrated in the case of Toward and probably Asgog Castle but in the local context this was an unlikely possibility.

The general plan was of a rectangular building of three or more storeys to which, in later castles, a wing was added to provide additional accommodation resulting in an 'L'–shaped plan. This wing was known as the jamb. The ground floor usually contained the kitchen, the cellars, and sometimes a pit prison. On the first floor there was a hall and perhaps at least one chamber. The Hall in some cases was furnished with a gallery. The upper floors contained further chambers. Frequently there were also small chambers within the thickness of the walls and on each storey there were latrines built within the wall thickness. They discharged by means of chutes down the wall face which are usually readily visible and must have been one of the less attractive features of the building when in occupation.

The communication between the floors was usually by a main newel stair and sometimes mural stairs from the first floor upwards. The newel stair ascended clockwise from the ground floor so that a defender would have his right sword-bearing arm outwards giving him maximum room for manoeuvre while his body would be partly protected by the central pillar. There is a tradition that the Kerr family trained their sons to be left-handed so that they would not be at a disadvantage when attacking up such a stair – hence the local name for a left-handed person as being 'corrie-fisted'. An interesting early example of specialisation.

Old Castle Lachlan could be described as a courtyard castle possibly developed from Innis Chonnel in Loch Awe or from Castle Sween, and modified to a restricted site. It provides considerably better accommodation than a tower house and is in a different tradition.

It should be borne in mind that although the ruined castles are now standing isolated and alone in the countryside, when they were occupied they would probably be surrounded at varying distances by the huts of their retainers and field workers. These would probably be rectangular structures, built of timber or turf and thatched – perhaps with heather. As they were built of destructible materials nothing remains to show evidence of their existence.

Most of the castles that remain even as ruins in Cowal were built by the chiefs of branches of the Campbells. Only Toward, Castle Lachlan and Dunderave belonged to other families. As will be seen from the chapter on 'Families' by the mid-14th century the Campbells had started to acquire land in Cowal and by the 18th and 19th centuries owned most of the estates. Each Campbell family would have a 'seat' in his

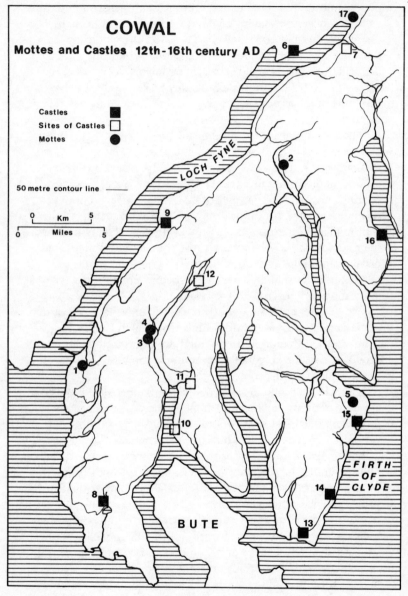

7. Castles and mottes

own territory but as only a few of these would be built in stone, only the ruins of a few of the stone castles remain to be seen in the 20th century.

Mottes

Sites worth visiting are marked with an asterisk.

1.   *Cnoc Mhic Eoghainn, Ballimore, Otter Ferry
NR 922 832

A dramatic steep-sided mound on the shores of Loch Fyne 100m S.W. of Ballimore House. There is probably a recent causeway to the summit on which there are two 19th century burial enclosures of the Campbells of Otter.

2.   *Balliemeanoch, Strachur
NS 102 999

A rectangular, flat-topped mound close to the junction of an unclassified road with the A815, 700m S.S.W. of Balliemeanoch farmhouse. There are traces of a bank on the N.E. edge of the summit and the remains of a building of 15th/16th century date.

3.   *Achanelid, Glendaruel
NS 006 873

A rectangular earthen mound consisting of a tree covered platform 500m S. of Auchanelid farmhouse surrounded by the remains of a ditch on the S. & W. sides. Remains of two buildings on the summit.

4.   *Dun an Oir, Achanelid, Glendaruel
NS 006 878

An artificially improved mound 100m W. of Auchanelid farmhouse and immediately across the river from the community hall. There is a slight scatter of stony debris around the edge of the summit.

5.   *Castle Crawford, Kirn
NS 179 786

The gorse covered remains of a rectangular platform are on the ground of the Cowal Golf course N.W. of Kirn. A well

defined ditch encloses the mound and on the summit a wall
probably dating from the 19th century.

17. Achadunan, Head of Loch Fyne
NN 200 135

This is a glacial mound which may have been utilised as a defensive mound as it is partially encircled with a ditch 10m. wide.
There are traces of walling but they may be the remains of a
field dyke. The mound has been eroded by the river making
its interpretation difficult. The farm name suggests that it is a
defended site.

Castles

Where possible, the castle has been linked with its family.

6. *Dundarave Castle, Cairndow MACNAUGHTON
NN 143 096

This 16th century tower house stands on Dunderave Point
about 5.8km from the head of Loch Fyne between the A83
and the loch. The castle is an 'L' plan tower built of rubble
masonry with sandstone dressings on exposed margins and
may incorporate material from an earlier building. It has four
main storeys and a garret. An $1^1/2$ storey addition enclosing
the N. and S. angles of the courtyard was built in the 20th
century designed to harmonise with the tower. The original
doorway is set in the S.E. wall of the stair turret. The internal
arrangement follows the conventional plan of that date – a
ground-floor kitchen and cellars; a first-floor hall and
chamber, and further chambers on the upper-floors of the
main block and wing, all served by the main newel stair.
There are further stairs linking the ground- and first-floor and
the hall and a second-floor chamber. There have been a series
of alterations to the original plan both in the 17th century and
in the 1911-12 restoration. .

The castle was erected by John MacNaughton in 1598 and
remained in occupation until the early 19th century but by the
middle of the century it had become a roofless shell. It was
restored and extended in 1911–12 under the direction of Sir
Robert Lorimer. It is now in private occupation.

Dunderave was the original of the 'Castle Doom' of Neil Munro's novel.

7. Ardkinglas, Cairndow CAMPBELL
NN 175 102

The castle was demolished prior to 1798. It was a Campbell castle and appears to have been situated about 150m. S. of the present Ardkinglas House. There are no traces extant.

8. *Asgog Castle, Millhouse, Kames LAMONT
NR 946 705

The shattered remains of this late medieval tower house are on the N.W. shore of Loch Asgog. It can be approached by a track which leads from a fieldgate on the left side of the Kames-Kilfinan road, 500m. north of Millhouse.

The tower measured about 14.3m by 10.3m before its destruction and is now in a dangerous state. It was of rubble construction with sandstone dressings in some openings. It consisted of a vaulted ground floor and probably two upper storeys. There are two mural chambers and a dog-leg stair to the first floor. There is a short section of a mural stair in the S.W. gable which may have led to the wallhead.

This castle is first recorded in 1581 and was held by the Lamonts until it was besieged by Campbell of Ormsary in 1646. It was surrendered on a safe conduct which was promptly violated, many of the defenders being massacred in Dunoon. The tower was then burnt and no effort has been made to restore it. THIS BUILDING IS DANGEROUS AND SHOULD NOT BE APPROACHED.

9. *Old Castle Lachlan, Strathlachlan MACLACHLAN
NS 005 952

The ruins of this castle are on a low promontory on the N. side of Lachlan Bay. The present approach is by a ramp of the 16th-17th century leading to the entrance archway. The castle consists of a quadrangular enclosure divided into two ranges by a narrow transverse central court. It was probably built in the early 15th century. It is largely of rubble construction with sandstone quoins and there was extensive

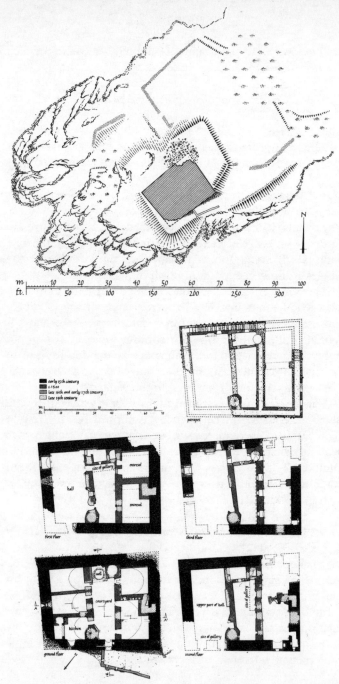

Figure 9.   Castle Lachlan

refacing of the walls about 1890. There is evidence of windows which have now been blocked.

The buildings of the S.W. range had three main storeys and a garret. The ground floor consisted of two cellars and a kitchen, all opening off the court. Above that, there was a hall which had a fireplace on the W. wall and which was entered from a newal stair. The third floor probably had two rooms, the fireplace of one survives. There was access from this floor and that above to the little chambers in the N.W. wing at the end of the courtyard and, through them, to the N.E. range. Access to the garret range and the wall walk was by the newal stair.

The N.W. wing fills the N.W. end of the courtyard and comprises a stair tower and a well with small rooms above and the site of a gallery at the first-floor level. The stair tower provided the only means of access to the upper floors of the N.E. range directly from the courtyard.

The N.E. range comprised two transversely vaulted cellars, each containing an entresol floor at ground level, and above that two floors, each of two rooms and a garret floor. The second floor rooms had a gallery facing on to the courtyard.

A charter dated 1314 was granted by Gilaspec Mac-Loughlan from a Castle Lachlan, which was probably the forerunner of the present ruin. The ruin is still owned by the MacLachlan family although not occupied after 1790 when only the N.E. range was roofed. The new Castle was built at this date and the old Castle was then allowed to fall into disrepair. The N. and S. angles collapsed some time after 1890. A local tradition states that the Castle was fired upon from the sea after Culloden in 1746

10. Eilean Dearg, Loch Riddon CAMPBELL
NS 008 770

The fragmentary remains of this castle occupy a small island known locally as 'One Tree Island'. It lies 150m. from the E. shore of Loch Riddon and 11.2km N. of the Burnt Islands in the Kyles of Bute. It is thought that it was a tower of 14th-15th century date, possible resembling Castle Stalker in Appin. It was blown up in 1685 by the same government force that burned Carrick Castle (No. 16).

The site is heavily overgrown with nettles but portions of shattered masonry are visible. Excavation revealed a massive rhomboidal tower, a possible hall range and a chapel. A quantity of musket flints and balls were recovered along with forty gaming counters.

The castle is recorded as being held in the 1440s by Campbell of Loch Awe but was in the possession of Campbell of Ormidale until its destruction.

11.   Achnabreac, Loch Riddon CAMPBELL
NS 019 814

The traditional site is a rectangular platform adjacent to Achnabreac farm house bounded by a 25m. length of revetment wall. It was a Campbell castle which was last occupied about the first decade of the 18th century and had disappeared by 1870.

12.   Garvie, Glendaruel CAMPBELL
NS 036 903

The site is traditionally immediately W. of Garvie farmhouse but there are no identifiable remains. It was possibly a Campbell tower house castle.

13.   *Toward Castle, Toward LAMONT
NS 118 678

The ruins of this, the principal castle of the Lamont family, are situated in the grounds and to the E. of the modern Castle Toward, about 150m from the shore

The castle was basically an oblong tower house standing on a promontory down which much of the masonry collapsed. The tower was probably built in the mid-15th century and associated with it is a courtyard with gatehouse. A hall and kitchen buildings ranged on the east of the court may date from the late 16th to the early 17th centuries. However local tradition calls the gateway 'Queen Mary's Gate' implying that the hall house may belong to the mid-16th century. The masonry is lime mortared rubble with sandstone dressings.

The tower is 11.8m by 8.8m. surviving to a height of about 13m. There were three main storeys and a part basement. The

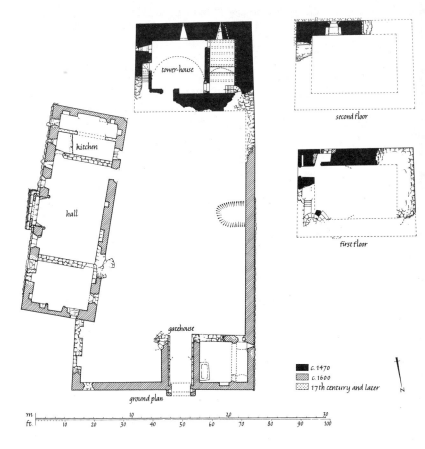

second floor

first floor

tower-house

kitchen

hall

gatehouse

■ c.1470
▨ c.1600
▨ 17th century and later

ground plan

N

Figure 10. Toward Castle

principal entrance appears to have been on the first floor in the
E. wall. The ground floor consists of two vaulted chambers
both of which contain mural stairs leading to the first floor.

The E. range consists of the lower storey of a possibly two-
storeyed building, the lower storey measuring 20.5m by 7.7m.
It is divided into three compartments, a chamber, a hall and a
kitchen. The hall has a large fireplace and there is a fireplace
arch and a slop sink in the kitchen. The remains of an external
stair can be seen.

The N. range consists of the gatehouse passage with on
one side a bakehouse and on the other, a chamber with the
remains of a newal stair. There is an enclosure wall
completing the courtyard.

A crown charter of 1472 confirms John Lawmond in the
barony of Inveryne. The towerhouse probably dates from about
then. Queen Mary of Scotland was entertained here in 1563.
In 1646 the castle was assaulted by Campbell of Ardkinglass
with troops and cannon and was surrendered by Sir James
Lamont on honourable terms. They were promptly violated
and the garrison was taken to Dunoon and massacred in
Dunoon churchyard. The castle was then plundered and burnt.

Parts of the structure appear to have been repaired in the
19th century and further excavation and consolidation took
place in 1970.

14.   *Knockamillie Castle, Innellan CAMPBELL
    NS 152 710

300m N.W. and above Innellan Pier there are the remains of
the S. wall of Knockamillie Castle. The wall is 7m. long and
7m. high. A wall which abuts this at right angles is comparatively modern and was built to prevent the collapse of the
original fragment. The building dates from after 1590 and
possession of the Campbells of Achnabreac.

15.   *Dunoon Castle STEWART: a Royal castle under
guardianship of the CAMPBELLS
    NS 175 763

The ruins occupy the summit of the rocky mound which may
be scarped motte, to the S.W. of Dunoon Pier. The few

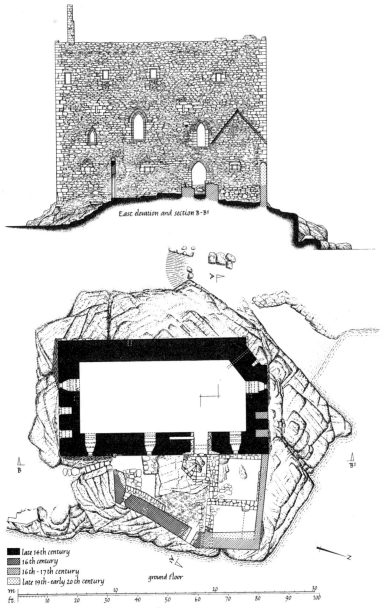

East elevation and section B-B¹

late 14th century
16th century
16th-17th century
late 19th-early 20th century

ground floor

Figure 11. Carrick Castle

visible remains comprise portions of the curtain wall enclosing an area 26m. by 18m. There is an entrance gateway close
to the W. angle. The curtain wall has been largely rebuilt in
modern times. There are recent concrete and brick foundations on the summit as it was used for both gun and
searchlight emplace-ments in the two World Wars.

The castle existed prior to 1250 and became a Crown
Castle when the Stewarts came to the throne in the late 14th
century. (See the Stewart Family). In 1419 an Act of
Parliament provided that 'the Castle of Dunnion should in all
time coming be the property of the heir to the Scottish
Throne'. A grant by James III in 1472 gave Colin, 'Count of
Ergill' custody of the 'Castle of Dunune' with power of
appointing constables necessary for keeping the said castle. In
1924 the Campbells of Dunoon Estate granted a feu to the
Town Council but retained their rights to the Captaincy and
custody of the Castle, on behalf of the Duke of Argyll.

The castle is shown in Pont's map of 1590 as a
conventional tower. It was last occupied about 1650 but was
finally plundered for building material when the Castle House
was built in 1820.

16.   *Carrick Castle, Loch Goil CAMPBELL
    NS 194 944

This castle is situated on the W. shore of Loch Goil 2.5km.
from the mouth of the loch. It is a large tower of probably the
14th century measuring 33m. by 28m and the walls stand to
their full height of between 14.5m and 17m. It is of rubble
masonry with sandstone quoins. It contained two principal
floors above an undercroft and there are no windows up to
the first floor on the landward side. The windows are very
varied in design and some of them have been altered. There
are mural stairs in the E. wall rising to the second floor and
the wall walk. The first floor was probably divided into a
lobby and a large hall, and the second floor into three
chambers of which the central may have contained an
oratory. Both the walls and the parapets have been heavily
restored and refaced. There are latrine chutes on both end
walls.

The castle was defended on the landward side by a deep ditch with a drawbridge spanning it. At one time this was defended by a wall and two small towers but there are now no traces of any of these features. There is a barmkin defending the present entrance on the E. wall of the tower which was probably rebuilt in the 16th century.

The castle was in the possession of the Campbells by 1424 and Mary Queen of Scots stayed in it for a night in 1563. The castle was burned in 1685 by Captain Hamilton of the frigate 'Kingfisher' at the time of the Argyll rebellion but the ownership remained with the Argyll estates until the present owner acquired it with the intention of restoring it as a residence.

CHURCHES

From the 12th to 19th centuries

When considering Cowal churches there are particular problems. Many of the existing pre-20th century churches are built on sites which have had previous ecclesiastical buildings on them – in some cases going back to Early Christian times. The existing buildings may incorporate structure or materials from one or more of these earlier buildings. In addition, particularly with grave slabs, materials may be re-used from buildings which were not on that site. The earlier construction may be completely masked by later work or surface treatments. Harling and plaster covers a wealth of evidence. The earliest churches which are intact are all post-Reformation but some comparatively modern churches, particularly Victorian ones, have been built in an archaic style, which, if early material has been incorporated in the structure, can deceive the casual visitor.

The dedications of many of the churches are to saints who are somewhat shadowy figures. It is worth remembering that, in the Celtic Church, the term 'saint' was synonymous with 'holy man' or 'holy woman' and did not have its modern connotation. Churches were dedicated to saints with which there was no local association. Aedan, to whom Kilmodan was dedicated (mo Aeden = my Aiden), is an Irish saint of whom little is known and Finan was a bishop of Lindisfarne who died in 661 AD and to whom several churches are dedicated. The preface to the chapter on Early Christian Sites is equally applicable to this chapter.

The transition from the Celtic church to the Roman Church was probably a very gradual one. The church buildings were in the gift of the local landowner who effectually appointed the priest and, as the Roman Church increased its authority in Scotland, more and more priests would follow the Roman Rite. In addition, from the 11th century onwards, it became fashionable to donate the patrimony of a church (and its revenues) to a monastery or, at a later date, to a collegiate church on condition that masses were said in perpetuity for the souls of the donor and his family. In the case of many of

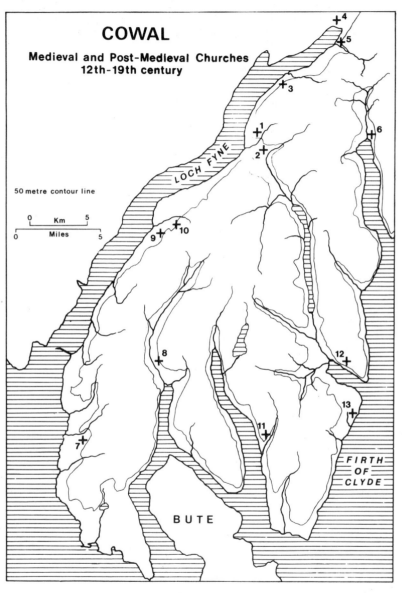

COWAL

**Medieval and Post-Medieval Churches
12th-19th century**

50 metre contour line

0   Km   5

0   Miles   5

LOCH FYNE

BUTE

FIRTH
OF
CLYDE

8. Churches

the local landowners their consciences made this an attractive
proposition. Two churches, Kilfinan and Kilmun, were
granted to the Cluniac Abbey of Paisley; Kilmodan was
granted to the Praemonstratensian Priory of Whithorn. It
must be stressed that it is extremely unlikely that the monks
took any active part in the running of these churches. Their
involvement would be as landlords, maintaining the fabric,
collecting the revenues and the appointing of a chaplain who
would almost certainly not be a monk.

It is outwith the scope of this book to go into detail on
Scottish Church history but it should not be forgotten that it
is very different from that of England. In the first instance the
Reformation came twenty-five years later in Scotland and was
very unevenly enforced. There were still monks singing their
offices in the 1590s and the Reformation never reached some
of the outer isles. The Reformation was, in the beginning, to
Episcopacy and only subsequently to Presbyterianism. It
should also be remembered that the Presbyterian Church was
itself split by the Disruption of 1843 when over a third of the
Ministers left the Established Church to form the Free Church.
The latter event had considerable repercussions in Cowal as
quite a few of the Cowal ministers signed the Deed of
Demission and took their congregations with them out of the
Church of Scotland to form new Free Church congregations.
As most of the Free Churches eventually rejoined the
Established Church in 1929 there was an excess of church
buildings many of which are now re-used for other purposes,
or have been demolished or unfortunately may be derelict.

It has been difficult to decide, for the reasons which are
given in the first paragraph, which churches should be
included in this book. It is not practicable to consider dates as
a sole criterion. It has been decided that if the church is
included in the Argyll Inventory of the R.C.A. & H.M.S. Vol.
7, then it should be described in this book. This may have
resulted in a church being omitted but we hope that we have
mentioned all the churches of archaeological significance in
Cowal and that the reader will understand our difficulties.
Some of the information found in Vol. 7 may be described in
Chapter 6 – 'The Coming of Christianity'.

Church Sites

The sites of nearly all of the churches described below, are also described in the gazetteer of the Early Christian Chapter.

At every site in this section, except for No 2, there are foundations, upstanding ruins, or a building to be seen.

1. Strachur Parish Church, Strachur
   NN 095 015

The church is in the centre of the village on the N. side of the street. It is a rectangular building with the vestry projecting from the centre of the S. wall. It is of rubble construction with sandstone quoins. It was built in 1789 and extensively rebuilt in 1902-3. The church has a bird cage belfry and there is gallery.

There was a church on the site in 1642 which was described as ruinous in 1698. There are medieval grave slabs built into the outer walls of the church which are said to come from the lost chapel at NN 100 005. The nearly round graveyard contains some interesting post-Reformation gravestones.

2. Chapel, Strachurmore, Strachur
   NN 100 005

The site of this chapel is believed to be on the W. bank of the River Cur 500 m S.W. of Strachurmore farm house. No trace remains but the field is known as the Chapel Field. It may be associated with the adjacent motte at NS 102 999.

3. Chapel, St. Catherine's
   NN 121 073

The remains of this late medieval chapel are about 120m from the shore of Loch Fyne above the old ferry slip. There is a quarry extending to within a few metres of the W. wall. The turf grown outline of the walls survive to about 0.5m high. The building was divided in two by a transverse wall. The chapel was in existence in 1466 and probably remained so until the early 17th century

4.   Kilmorich Parish Church, Cairndow
   NN 180 107

This church is situated about 100m from the entrance to Ardkinglas estate and was built in 1816 to replace a building of
possible 18th-century date. It is a harled and white-washed octagonal building with sandstone quoins, a pyramidal roof and a
W. tower. There is a gallery which is entered from the tower.

   There is a medieval font, a grave slab and a damaged cross
head of possibly 12th-13th century date in the church all of
which presumably came from the old parish church.

5.   Kilmorich Old Parish Church, Clachan, Cairndow
   NN 189 128

The site of this medieval church is in the burial ground 200m
north of Clachan farm – now the Oyster Bar. A turf mound in
the centre of the burial ground possibly marks the foundations of a wall. The church was first recorded in about 1246
in a grant to the Augustinian Abbey of Inchaffray. There are
three medieval grave slabs in the churchyard.

6.   The Three Holy Brethren, Lochgoilhead
   NN 198 014

The church is situated in Lochgoilhead about 80m from the
N. shore of the loch. The building may incorporate some of
the fabric of a late medieval church. A north aisle was added
in the 18th century and a session house in the 19th. The walls
are of rubble masonry harled externally, with sandstone
quoins. Internally the church is 'T' plan with a gallery in the
W. arm. The pulpit was brought from Kiltearn, Ross and
Cromarty and probably dates from 1791. The E. arm of the
'T', the former chancel, contains an early 16th century
monument which incorporates the blocked entrance to a now
demolished burial vault.

   The dedication to the 'Three Holy Brethren' whose
identity is unknown, is in a mandate of 1392 and the revenues
of the parish were assigned in 1441 to the collegiate church of
Kilmun. The church at that time was stated to be in a poor
state and was probably then extensively rebuilt, as happened
also in 1644.

There are Early Christian and Medieval carved stones in the church and interesting post-reformation gravestones in the grave yard. There is also an early sundial.

7. Kilfinan Parish Church
NR 934 788

This much altered medieval church stands beside the village. The road actually cuts across the churchyard. The church was first recorded in the 13th century and the present church may follow the outline of the earlier building with the addition of the Lamont aisle, which was built in 1633, and may itself incorporate earlier work. The church was rebuilt in 1759 and extensively restored in 1881-2. The external surface of the building is harled which conceals any early work. There is a ground floor burial vault below the Lamont aisle which is entered from the outside of the church.

The church is first recorded in 1253 and was granted to the Cluniac Abbey of Paisley. It was stated to be ruinous in 1690.

There are Early Christian and Medieval monuments in the Lamont aisle and post-reformation gravestones in the churchyard.

8. Kilmodan Parish Church
NR 995 841

This church is situated to the W. of the Clachan of Glendaruel. It was built in 1783 replacing an older, possibly medieval, church. A chaplaincy is recorded as early as 1250 and by 1425 it had become a prebend of the diocese of Argyll. The revenues are recorded as being annexed to Whithorn Priory.

The present church is of a 'T' plan with walls of harled rubble having sandstone quoins and a hipped and slated roof. There are three galleries for the Campbells of Glendaruel, the Campbells of Ormidale and the Campbells of South Hall which are entered from within the church. The octagonal pulpit may be original. The building was extensively renovated in the 1980s.

In the corner of the churchyard there is a lapidarium containing the largest group of medieval grave slabs in Cowal. Most of the stones are dated to the 14th and 15th centuries and

belong to a school of carvers which was centred near Loch
Awe.

9. Kilmorie, Strathlachlan
NS 010 951

The fragmentary remains of this medieval church are in an
oval graveyard on the S. bank of the Strathlachlan River
300m past the caravan site on the B8000 from Newton to
Tighnabruaich. The remains of the church consist of the E.
wall to which is attached the roofless burial aisle of the
Maclachlans of Maclachlan. The walls are of rubble with
dressings of schist and sandstone. The walls of the burial aisle
have marble memorial tablets.

The church is first recorded in 1543 and the burial aisle
was probably added about 1592. The last records of repairs to
the church were before 1728 and it was in its present
condition in 1840.

The cross in the churchyard is probably 15th century; all
the other stones are later than 1800.

The name suggests a dedication to the Blessed Virgin
Mary but it may be to St Maelrubha, a monk of Bangor, Co.
Down who founded a monastery in Applecross, Wester Ross.

10. Parish Church, Strathlachlan
NS 021 958

This rectangular building of harled rubble was built about
1792. It has a birdcage belfry and the internal furnishings are
mostly of recent date.

11. Parish Church, Inverchaolain, Loch Striven
NS 090 753

The present building is situated N. of the Inverchaolain Burn
and 130m. from the loch side. This building dates from 1912
replacing a building of 1812 which itself is believed to have
had two predecessors. The parish is thought to date from
about 1230 and was at one time granted to the Trinitarian
House of Fail.

There are medieval slabs in the church and churchyard.

12. Parish Church, Kilmun
NS 166 820

The church stands beside the A880 road from Dunoon to Ardentinny, in Kilmun village. The present building dates from 1841, occupying the site of the collegiate church of 1442, the W. tower of which still stands 4m. W. of the present building. The site has been occupied by an ecclesiastical building since the middle of the 13th century.

The 15th-century tower stands 9.5m high to the wall-head and is built of rubble with sandstone quoins. There is a vaulted ground floor and a newal stair in the S.W. angle giving access to two upper floors and a garret chamber in the roof. The N. and S. walls of the tower show the remains of the side walls of the nave of the former church with the raggle for the nave roof on the E. wall. The old church was extensively renovated in 1688 and again in 1790 before being demolished in 1841.

The Argyll Mausoleum of 1795 remodelled in 1891, which is situated E. of the church, replaced the former burial vault at the N.E. end of the old church.

The church of Kilmun is first recorded in a charter of about 1232-41 in which the patronage was granted to the Cluniac Abbey of Paisley but there are no records of the Abbey exercising any rights. It was elevated to a collegiate church of a provost and five chaplains in 1441. The church was described as being wholly ruinous in 1660 but was apparently repaired in 1688.

The churchyard contains a large number of medieval and post-reformation grave stones many of which have extremely interesting inscriptions. There is a mortsafe and a watch house of probable 19th-century origins. Dr Elizabeth Blackwell, the first female doctor to be registered in Britain, is buried in the graveyard.

13. Parish Church, Dunoon
NS 174 766

The church stands at the head of Kirk St. W. of Dunoon pier and 200m N. of the Castle on the same contour.

This Perpendicular Gothic building was built in 1816,

enlarged in 1834 and further altered in 1839 and 1911. It is built of white sandstone rubble with sandstone dressings and has a tower and galleries.

A medieval church dedicated to St. Mary is recorded from 1270 onwards and a church was described as 'the Parish Church of the Blessed Virgin Mary' in 1402. A building on the site, probably a later church still was said to be 'beyond repair' in 1812.

TOWNSHIPS AND COMMUNICATIONS
From the 12th (?) to the 19th centuries.

Townships

The remains of the stone-built townships which are widely scattered on the lower hillslopes throughout Cowal and the West of Scotland are unlikely to belong to a period earlier than 1700–1750. Houses constructed from turf which may have preceded the stone ones in Medieval times leave no surface evidence. It is probable, though, that the turf houses were on the same sites as the later stone buildings although isolated turf foundations are known on the moors. It is also probable that as long as the castles were occupied many huts and houses would cluster around them. Building in turf was prohibited by law in the late 15th century as turf houses were impoverishing the ground. Nevertheless it is thought from excavation and survey that building in stone did not become general until about the early 18th century.

The townships were multiple-tenancy farms – the rent being paid in kind to the chief or his tacksman – by the families who lived on and worked the surrounding land. A visit to Auchindrain, the open air folk museum about 7 miles south of Inveraray on Loch Fyneside, will illustrate the life in such a township of the 18th and 19th centuries.

Potatoes were the main crop and staple diet but oats and barley were grown, all were cultivated on the run-rig system. Each family would own a few cows which would be pastured together and would require constant herding as the ground was unfenced. In the winter the animals would be kept indoors and hand fed; in the summer they would be taken to the 'sheiling' – the high pasture on the hills above the township – to take the beasts away from the growing crops and to give them the advantage of fresh new grass.

The people would live almost solely on their own produce though a small amount of cash might be found from the occasional sale of some or even one of the black cattle. The heifers would join the cattle from other townships and be driven west and south by a professional drover who took the cattle droves to the market at Crieff or Falkirk. There the beasts would be sold and many would be driven on over the Border eventually arriving at the cattle market in London.

Much time and effort would be given to the cutting, carrying and stacking of peat which would be the chief source of fuel. Charcoal, used for particular processes, was also made from peat.

After 1707 when the Scottish Parliament ceased to exist the ancient way of life gradually disappeared. Money (currency) became an essential commodity and many of the chiefs became landlords (often absent ones) rather than father-figures who lived amongst and shared the life of their people. The 1715 and 1745 risings hastened this Anglicisation and sheep were introduced to the hills to give much-needed cash to the landowners.

In Cowal there is no tradition or knowledge of actual 'Clearance' of the hills for the sheep as in the Highlands but it happened. The townships dwellers could not raise the rent money needed to pay for their ancient land rights. Many went overseas, others gradually drifted to the growing towns – Glasgow, and Greenock – which were rapidly expanding as industry developed. Eventually the townships were deserted – some were simply abandoned – Glaic (54), Gortein (12); a few were 'improved' firstly and later abandoned in the late 19th and early 20th century – Kildalven (14), Ardgadden (6); and some became single tenancy farms – Auchamore, and Ardnadam (neither listed in gazetteer).

When visiting a township it is worth looking for the corn kiln. This appears now as a hump of ground often with a hollow on the top (perhaps about 2m high and 3 to 4m diameter). These were the kilns where the grain was parched to dry it before grinding in a hand quern. A fire was lit at the outer end of a flue which carried the heat into the kiln which was hollow internally. The grain lay on a rack stretched across the hollow interior. Practically every township had a corn kiln; some had two.

Communications

From earliest times the principal means of travel both to Cowal and within Cowal was by water. The Clyde together with Lochs Long, Striven, Riddon, Fyne, Goil, the Holy Loch and the Kyles of Bute so intersect the peninsula, that nowhere is more than eight miles from the sea. In addition, Loch Eck was a convenient route which bisected Cowal and provided an easy passage from the Clyde at the Holy Loch to Loch Fyne and thence onward to Knapdale and the islands of the West. This was the route that was taken by Mary, Queen of Scots, on her return from Inveraray to Dunoon in 1563.

Land communication was difficult. A few stretches of the bridle paths which are associated with the ruined townships and connecting ferry points can still be found and those are marked on Plan 10. However, many of these have recently been lost under afforestation. The few main routes were no more than pack pony tracks over difficult and boggy ground. The old tracks all crossed the hills taking the most direct line between landing stages and thence by boat across the water. The first document referring to the roads of Cowal is in a Minute of 1710 on the maintenance of a mountain track over the Bealach na Sreine between Dalilongart and Inverchaolain.

The line of the present road from Glen Lean (actually from Dunoon Ferry) over the Bealachandrain to Otter Ferry may follow one of the earliest land routes in Cowal as it crosses three hill ridges. The present back road (A 885) from Dunoon to Sandbank was built in 1801. Previously the old track which led to Otter Ferry passed along the west side of Loch Loskin and then through the gap to the west of Ardnadam Farm to Glen Lean.

By 1810 the road from Ardlamont Point to the military road over Rest and Be Thankful was completed but it is questionable to what extent it would have been fit for wheeled traffic. The section through Glen Kinglas and Glen Croe was built as a military road by General Caulfield in the last quarter of the 18th century as part of the programme to improve communications in the Highlands after the '45. This section through the Glens and round the head of Loch Fyne was built

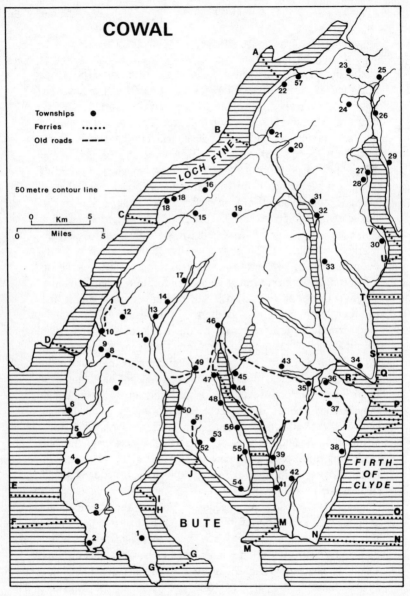

9. Settlements, ferries and tracks

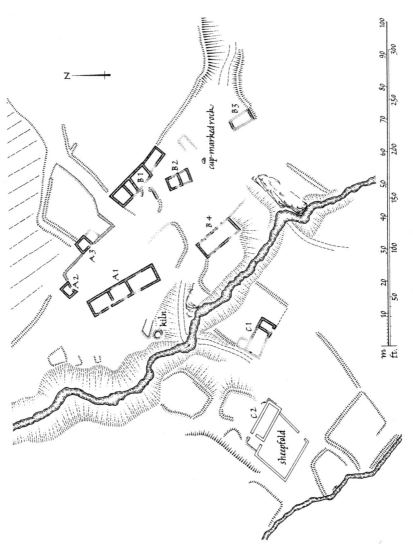

Figure 12 Kildalven Deserted Township

at the instigation of the Duke of Argyll to facilitate the movement of his troops between Inveraray and the lowlands and was
thus an important link in the pacification of the Highlands.

The shore road from Sandbank through Dunoon to
Innellan and Toward is very recent – sections were not built
until the 20th century. Many of the existing roads were not
metalled until after 1947 and parts of the road to
Tighnabruaich – A8003 – and the road to Colintraive – A886
– were constructed in the 1960s and 1970s.

The lack of roads until the 20th century resulted in a very
large number of ferries, some just rowing boats, but others
large enough to take cattle, horses and possibly carriages. In
some cases the passengers landed on an open beach, in
others, as at Otter Ferry, there is a well preserved quay and
ferry house dating from the end of the 18th century. Those
shown on Plan 10 do not pretend to be a complete
distribution as some of the former ferry sites are in doubt and
the landing places unidentifiable.

Some Deserted Settlements of Cowal and the Known Ferries

Settlements

These are a small number of the many settlements which must
have been scattered about Cowal in the 18th and 19th centuries and earlier. Those shown are those which have not been
rebuilt, those which are not now occupied and those which
have not been developed to become 20th century villages or
farms. Those marked with an asterisk are worth visiting.

1. *NR 986 673 Achadachoun Ardlamont.
2. *NR 930 678 Low Stillaig, Ardlamont.
3. NR 935 704 Derybruich, Millhouse.
4. *NR 925 712 Glennan. (Engulfed in forestry trees but
   well preserved.)
5. NR 922 758 Inveryne, foundations beside present
   farmhouse.
6. *NR 918 800 Ardgaddon, Kilfinan. (Two settlements
   close together – one older than the other.)
7. NR 946 805 Dalmunsaig, Kilfinan.

8. *NR 942 834 Unnamed – to N. of Bealachandrain road
at junction with Strone road.
Turf foundations and difficult to see;
spread on both sides of the burn.

9. *NR 940 844 House foundation beside earlier enclosure
NR 941 844 Turf house foundations on hill above

10. NR 939 852 Largiemore.

11. NR 991 854 Camquhart, Glendaruel – further turf-
walled rect. founds set along hillside.

12. *NR 957 879 Gortein, Lochfyneside.

13. NR 995 875 Eskachlachlan, Glendaruel.

14. *NS 017 889 Kildalven, Glendaruel – Other sites to N.
(Worth a visit to see the field terracing)

15. *NS 033 965 Feorline, Strathlachlan – behind and to E.
of present farm.

16. NS 057 987 Letters, Strachur.

17. NS 007 967 Kilbride, Strathlachlan (Now a farm)

18. *NS 022 981 Portindrain, Strathlachlan
*NS 019 976 Earlier Portindrain.

19. NS 095 966 Aucharbracaid, Glen Branter.

20. NN 113 011 Dufeorline.

21 *NN 104 025 Unnamed – house funds. to W. of river
and above road leading to television mast.

22. NN 099 048 Airidh a' Ghobhainn.

23. NN 174 062 Gleniarnbeg, Hell's Glen.

24. NN 180 042 Glenconichton, remains of township spread
over hillside, partly under forestation.

25. NN 204 063 Gleniarnmore – ruins stretch along hill.

26. NN 199 035 Tom a' Bhlair

27. NS 204 931 Lower Cormonachen, Loch Goil.

28. NS 191 967 Upper Cormonachen.

29. NS 209 979 Stuckbeg, Loch Goil.

30. NS 204 931 Ardnahein, Loch Goil

31. NS 132 965 Unnamed. (Cambusdhu?), Loch Eck.

32. NS 133 953 Stronhunsan, – all along Loch Eck side
are foundations of small structures.

33. NS 143 914 Ardnablaithaich, Loch Eck.

34. NS 168 830 Allt na Struthaig, various single foundations around

35. *NS 129 808 Gortnamhuinne, Glen Kin.
36. *NS 146 816 Old Dalinlongart (?) (Foundations to E. of Burial Ground)
37. NS 157 800   Finbracken, – behind Ardnadam Farm.
38. NS 164 747   Gerhallow.
39. NS 094 748   Tighnuilt, Loch Striven.
40. NS 093 741   Knockdhu.
41. *NS 096 721 Kilmarnock. (Immediately N.W. of Nato Base)
42. NS 115 728   Unnamed – in Glenfyne.
43. *NS 102 823 Cuilbuidhe, Glen Lean. (under power lines, on N.E. side of road, 500m. N.W. of junction of main road with Corrachaive farm road).
44. *NS 063 808 Bot nam Creagan, Loch Striven.
45. NS 064 828   Unnamed – settlement between burn and road, on very steep gradient.
46. NS 054 860   Unnamed – in Glen Laoigh, at head of Loch Striven
47. *NS 051 820 Stiallag, Loch Striven. (Worth seeing but difficult to reach)
48. *NS 061 786 Ardbeg, Loch Striven. (Worth seeing but difficult of access)
49. *NS 032 827 Tamhnich. (Can be seen from road in the right light. Look also from the road for curved rigs in the improved land below township.)
50. *NS 012 780 Ceardoch, Loch Riddon. (Below the new road in overgrown ground)
51. *NS 025 772 Ach na Sithean. (Can be seen from the road)
52. *NS 026 763 Unnamed.
53. NS 044 765   Unnamed, high above Ardentraive Farm.
54. *NS 075 716 Glaic at Strone Point. (Very worth while visiting as unimproved – an interesting survival. Access by forestry road to N.E.)

An 'improved' Glaic was built, probably in the 19th century, 400 yds above and to the N.W. There the houses were set in a row along the contour of the hill instead of into the hill. This

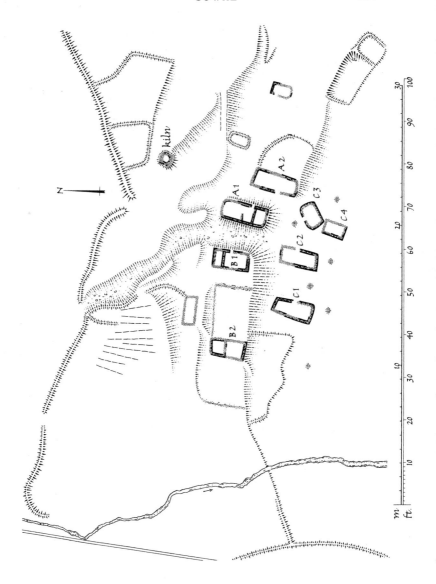

Figure 13. Strone Point Deserted Settlement

'new' township was completely destroyed during World War II as it was used for target practice by the Royal Navy.

55. NS 078 743   Coustonn
56. NS 074 765   Troustan
57. NN 144 080   Laglingarten

Ferries

A. NN 121 076   St Catherine's to Inveraray
B. NN 087 015   Strachur to Kenmore
C. NS 007 958   Just N. of Castle Lachlan to Brainport
D. NR 930 846   Otter to West Otter
E. NR 906 723   Barpuntaig to unidentified site N. of Stonefield Castle
F. NR 930 691   Port-a-Mhadaidh to Tarbert
G. NR 993 656   Ardlamont Ferry to unidentified site N. of Ettrick Bay
H. NR 982 696   Blair's Ferry to Kilmichael
I.   Another possible ferry N. of the above.
J. NS 032 745   Colintraive to Rhubodach
K. NS 077 742–NS 091 730   Coustonn to Brackley Point
L. NS 052 820–NS 070 789   Stiallag to (probably) Port na Curaich
M. NS 097 701   Port Lamont to Rothesay
N. NS 137 673   Toward to Skelmorlie
O. NS 146 697   Innellan to Wemyss Bay
P. NS 176 765   Dunoon to the Cloch
P. NS 185 780   Kirn to the Cloch
P. NS 186 792   Hunters Quay (Cammesreinach) to the Cloch
Q. NS 186 792–NS 195 818   Hunters Quay (Cammesreinach) to Blairmore
R NS 173 804–NS 174 808   Lazaretto Point to Gibb's Point or Graham's Point
S. NS 195 818   Blairmore to Cove (and Roseneath)
T. NS 188 873   Ardentinny to Coulport
U. NS 204 908   Knap to Portincaple
V. NS 193 945   Carrick to Portincaple.
W. NS 264 012   Coillessan to Glen Douglas (Beyond extent of map)

INDUSTRY IN COWAL

Cowal has always been a rural area and, even today, if one excludes the conurbation of Dunoon, what little industry exists, is confined to forestry, fish farming and the tourist trade.

There always has been what could be described as industrial enterprise on a very small scale. Bloomeries, where bog iron was smelted to give pure iron for the making of domestic tools is an example. The remains of these primitive furnaces are widespread and frequently disturbed by new forestry ploughing. Charcoal making was another domestic industry, and the pitsteads were also widespread.

In compiling the list of industrial sites, of necessity we have had to restrict mention to those enterprises employing a reasonable number of workers. Thus the bloomeries, the charcoal pits, the numerous water-powered mills, both threshing and meal, have been excluded. Similarly black-smiths, village carpenters and masons are not mentioned but this does not mean that they did not exist.

Specific mine workings are known to have existed at Kilfinan and Blairmore and there also records of workings at Strachur and Toward but none were worked commercially.

Fishing undoubtedly took place from various sites around the coast and there are records of a fishing industry at Strachur and at Newton but the lack of a harbour and adequate transport facilities must have restricted it to a small scale enterprise working from small boats which could be hauled up on to the beach. However at Strachur there is a bay which would give shelter and a base. It is of interest that at the Ardnadam site, – NS 163 791 – the latest use of the enclosure there, was in the late 19th or early 20th century. At that time there was, dug into the ground three hearths with converging gutters leading from the hearths to a central point where, it was thought, a metal container was balanced and in which fish may have been smoked. Fish smoking must have been a usual form of pre-servation and probably there were many more smoking sheds and smaller units for smoking fish, scattered around the area.

Ferries and transport are mentioned elsewhere in the book

and must have employed a considerable number of people. Cattle droving would also make an impact in the late summer and early autumn though the locals would not necessarily act as drovers. The ferries across Loch Fyne, across Loch Long and the Clyde would all be heavily used by the cattle droves on the way to the trysts at Crieff or at Falkirk. A gentleman from Sandbank who has recently died remembered from his childhood, seeing the long lines of cattle coming through Glen Lean.

Industrial sites – 18th, 19th and 20th centuries

1.   Clachaig Gunpowder works
NS 123 815

The site is among woodlands on the South side of the Dunoon-Colintraive road – B 836 – 2.5 km from Dalinlongart Farm and immediately to the East of the houses of Clachaig village.

This extensive complex of buildings dates from 1843-4 when Robert Sherrif commenced operations. The enterprise was bought by Curtiss & Harvey in 1856 who acquired more land and enlarged the factory. They also built what is now the village of Clachaig to house key workers. The factory finally closed in 1903 and the roofs of the buildings were removed to escape taxation.

The power used was entirely from water and there are the remains of the dam and sluice with a system of lades taking the water to the scattered process houses. A large overshot wheel was placed between each pair of process houses; the wheel pits are still obvious. There is also the track of a light railway which was carried on a bridge across the river, and girders of the bridge are still in place. Steam was used for heating and drying the powder and the pillars which carried the steam pipe can still be seen. Some of the buildings are double walled to limit blast in the case of an accident and, when the factory was working, the flat roofs of the buildings were constructed to hold water which would be immediately available to douse the contents of the building.

The powder was shipped by boats which were beached on the sand at Sandbank and the powder taken out to the boats at low tide in carts. This is the origin of the name 'the Sand Bank' which was the port of loading and the postal address for mail.

2. Millhouse Gunpowder Works, Millhouse Kames
NR 957 707

The site is in woodland to the east of the Kames-Kilfinan road – B 8000 – 300m North of the Millhouse crossroads. The entry is beside the bridge over the river.

Production in the works commenced in 1839 and finally ended in 1921. The materials for making the gunpowder and the finished product were transported by sea to and from the quay at Kames which is still known as the Powder Quay. One of the ships employed on this work was named appropriately, the 'Guy Fawkes'. As at Clachaig, Curtiss & Harvey built cottages for their key workers at Millhouse and Kames, most of which are still occupied. The gable ends of those cottages at Millhouse which face the factory were built without windows as a protection against blast.

There is a similar range of process buildings to those at Clachaig and, until 1914, water was the source of power. The system of lades is more complicated than at Clachaig with one lade being carried across another by an aquaduct. Steam power was first introduced as early as 1855 in case of frost and there were two engine houses with the power being transmitted by overhead wires and pulleys. There was also a light railway system and the abutments can still be seen, where several bridges crossed the stream.

Water was drawn from two reservoirs, still known as the Powder Lochs, on the east of the Millhouse-Kilfinan road (NR 95 74). The remains of the lade can be found on either side of the road leading towards Loch Asgog.

Associated with the gunpowder works there were saltpetre works at Kames and some of the buildings still exist in a much altered form.

3. Yachtyard, Robertson, Sandbank
NS 158 808

The side of this yard is on the outskirts of Sandbank on either side of the Dunoon-Glasgow road.

It consists of a complex of buildings some of which are wood built. There is a slipway with the remains of a traverser, a wooden jetty and a masting derrick. The buildings date from the late 19th century and the yard had a reputation for building high quality yachts including two America's Cup Challengers. 'Sceptre' was built in the late 1950s and in the early 1960s two others were built – one of which, 'Sovereign' was chosen as challenger.

The site is now semi-derelict and has recently been used as a scrap yard.

Previous to its use as a yachtyard the site was occupied by a distillery. One of the distillery buildings can still be seen on the south side of the A815 road at the extreme end of the complex.

4.   Yachtyard, Morris & Lorimers, Sandbank
NS 162 805

The site of this yard, until very recently, was used as a supply base for the American Navy. It is in Sandbank at the junction between the Dunoon-Sandbank coast road and the main Dunoon-Glasgow road.

'Lorimer's Yard' was not so active in yacht building as Robertson's but had a very good reputation for maintenance, particularly the slipping of large sailing and motor yachts. These were hauled up each winter and fitted out in the spring. Between the wars luxury steam yachts moored in the loch were serviced and the yard was the headquarters for the skippers and crews. The yard could slip yachts up to fourteen feet draught.

The only one of the original buildings which now remain is the shed now occupied by Blacks the carriers, which was built in 1950.

5.   Waukmill, Glendaruel
NR 999 827

The Waukmill was situated on the north side of the Tighnabruaich road – A 8003 – and on the west side of the bridge over the River Ruel. The site is now occupied by a cottage. There is mention of a waukmiller in Kilfinan Parish in the First Statistical Account of 1795.

6. Lazaretto Point, Sandbank
NS 172 803

The remains consist of a short length of wall and a tower. These are the sole remains of a quarantine station which was established about 1800. It is probable that the purpose was for the quarantine of goods, particularly cotton, and there was a range of store buildings and houses for the workers. It was discontinued about 1840-50 and the buildings demolished.

7. Copper Mines, Kilfinan
NR 935 786

Three copper mines were worked in the area between Kilfinan parish and Inveryne. They appear to have been more exploratory rather than a commercial enterprise, although some ore was extracted.

8. Limekilns, Kilfinan and Otter
NR 935 788 & 933 837

Two well preserved rubble-fronted, single-draw limekilns with brick linings and semi-circular arched draw holes are at these locations. The former is opposite Kilfinan Church but behind the old school; the latter is on the west side of the Tighnabruaich – Otter Ferry road (B 8000) about 200m south of its junction with the Glendaruel road. They are both of early 19th-century origin.

9. Glen Lean Distillery, Garrochoran
NS 115 812

A distillery was in operation here in the middle of the 19th century and some of the buildings were incorporated in the later farm.

10. Yachtyard, Port Driseach, Tighnabruaich
NR 993 740

This yard is still in existence although now only used for laying up and winter maintenance. It consists of a slip and steam winch for hauling boats out of the water (no longer in use) and a variety of sheds in varying states of repair.

11.   Lead and Silver Mines, Blairmore
NS 185 834

There are extensive workings which are said to go under
Blairmore Hill and which at one time emerged in Strath
Eachaig. Three portals exist of which the only one that is
open is behind Blairmore Farm. Debris from the mines form
fan deltas in Loch Long. The mines were worked, mainly by
Irish labourers, about 130 years ago but there are no records
of significant mineral recoveries.

TOURISM IN COWAL
An Epilogue

The advent of the tourist trade could be said to date from 1779 when Robert Reid's parents rented a farm house in Dunoon for the whole of the summer at a cost of fifty shillings (£2.50). It took a whole day until late in the evening for them to sail by private charter from the Broomielaw. Sixty-five years later the same journey could be done in under three hours at a cost of one shilling (5p). The ease and cheapness by which it was possible for the citizens of Glasgow to reach Cowal by steamship from the centre of Glasgow explains the enormous expansion of the Clyde coast communities. Most were tiny villages or perhaps comprised only two or three cottages when Queen Victoria ascended the throne.

The increasing wealth of the Glasgow merchants made it possible for them to build holiday houses to which they migrated for the summer months with their numerous children. The expansion of the railway to Greenock, and then to Gourock and Wemyss Bay, made it perfectly feasible for the 'pater familias' to commute to his office in Glasgow every day. It was, for example, possible for a person to catch the steamer at Colintraive at 7.00 a.m., have breakfast on the boat, and be in Glasgow by 9.00 a.m.

The Castle House in Dunoon, set above the pier and between the mound of the Castle and the Parish Church, was built as a summer residence by James Ewing M.P. the Lord Provost of Glasgow in 1822. It is said to be the first of the summer houses built in Dunoon. There were also a large number of houses built for summer letting both by local landowners and Glasgow entrepreneurs. Men like James Hunter of Hafton, who built piers at Dunoon and Hunters Quay, took a prominent part in this development. Between 1822 and 1845 there were 220 feu charters granted by the Milton estate alone. A similar process of expansion took place all round Cowal. It could be truly said that, for the vast majority of the Glaswegians, Cowal, with Bute, Arran and the Ayrshire Coast, was their holiday playground.

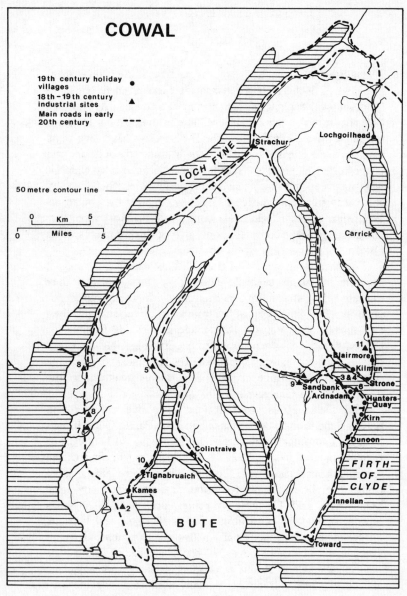

COWAL

19th century holiday villages ●

18th–19th century industrial sites ▲

Main roads in early 20th century – – –

50 metre contour line ———

Km 0 5

Miles 0 5

LOCH FYNE

Strachur

Lochgoilhead

Carrick

11

Blairmore

Kilmun

1

3 & 4

Strone

9

Sandbank

6

Ardnadam

Hunters Quay

Kirn

Dunoon

8

5

8

7

Colintraive

10

Tignabruaich

Kames

2

BUTE

FIRTH OF CLYDE

Innellan

Toward

10. Present day towns, villages and roads

This frenzied activity came to an abrupt halt on 4th August, 1914. The depression that followed the first World War not only prevented the resumption of this type of development but also the market for it.

Between the wars Cowal remained a favourite holiday destination for many Glaswegians as the number of hotels and boarding houses bear witness. There was still a remnant remaining of the great fleet of paddle and turbine steamers which throughout the century had collected people each morning from the piers of the Firth and transported them as if in their own private yachts to see the glory of the West of Scotland.

An industry which has now however completely disappeared was the building and hiring of rowing boats and small motor boats to visitors. Both bays at Dunoon and the bays of the smaller villages were alive with small boys and girls and older people too, rowing small dinghies, fishing and bathing. The boat hirers spent the winter building boats, not only for themselves, but also for sale. Many of these found owners far from Cowal and Dunoon-built dinghies are still being found in other areas of the country.

From the 1950s onwards the holiday destinations for the vast majority of British people have changed to more exotic climes for which, it is probable, the cost of accommodation and transport in this country is largely to blame. Cowal is still just as beautiful as it was in 1914 and it is hoped that this book will encourage visitors to look a little beyond the beauty to the history of the area – a centre of human activity from the earliest times.

BIBLIOGRAPHY AND FURTHER READING

Bannerman, J. W. M., *Studies in the History of Dalriada* (Scottish Academic Press, 1974)

Coles, Bryony and John, *People of the Wetlands.* (Vol 106 of 'Ancient Peoples and Places') (Guild Publishing, 1989)

Finlay, Ian, *Columba* (Gollancz, 1979)

Henshall, Audrey, *Chambered Tombs of Scotland Vol. 2* (Edinburgh University Press, 1972)

Keppie, Lawrence, *Scotland's Roman Remains* p. 4 (John Donald Publishers Ltd, 1985)

Kirby, D. P., *'Who are the Scots?'* General Editor – Gordon Menzies. B.B.C., 1971.

MacGibbon, D. and Ross, T., *The Castellated and Domestic Architecture of Scotland,* 5 vols. (Mercat Press, 1887-1892)

McLean, Angus, *The Dunoon of Old,* (pp 15-22) *The Place Names of Cowal* (Dunoon Observer)

Marshall, D. N., Proc. of the Soc. of Antiqs. of Scot. (1977-78. vol. 109, pp 36-74.

Morris, Ronald W. B., *The Prehistoric Rock Art of Argyll* (Dolphin Press, 1977)

Morrison, Ian, *Landscape with Lake Dwellings* (Edinburgh University Press, 1985)

Rennie, Elizabeth, *Glasgow Archaelogical Journal Vol 11* pp 13-38 (1984) (Further publication pending)

Ritchie, Anna, *Scotland B.C.* (H.M.S.O, 1988)

Ritchie, Anna and Breeze, David, *Invaders of Scotland* (H.M.S.O.)

Ritchie, Graham and Anna, *Scotland: archaeology and early history* (Edinburgh University Press, 1991)

Tabraham, T., *Scottish Castles and Fortifications* (H.M.S.O., 1986)

Watson, William J., *History of the Celtic Place Names of Scotland* (Birlinn Ltd, 1993)

For the more detailed information about many of the sites and for a more thorough discussion about the history and pre-history of the area:

Argyll Vol. 6 – *The Pre-Historic and Early Historic Monuments of Mid-Argyll and Cowal.*

Vol. 7 – *The Later Monuments of Mid-Argyll and Cowal*
Published by H.M.S.O.

Elizabeth B. Rennie, Upper Netherby, Kirn, Dunoon.

INDEX

Also available from

BIRLINN

ILLUSTRATED GAELIC-ENGLISH DICTIONARY

Edward Dwelly

Published between 1901 and 1911 the Dwelly Dictionary is to Gaelic as the Oxford English Dictionary is to English. An extraordinary achievement by an extraordinary man, it remains the standard Gaelic dictionary and reference book, used by learners and laymen alike.

This is its first paperback edition and has enhanced and enlarged reproduction.

ISBN 1 874744 04 1
216 x 138mm, 1056 pages
Paperback £12.99

THE CELTIC PLACE NAMES
OF SCOTLAND

W. J. Watson

First published in 1926, this remains the greatest source book
ever written on the place names of Scotland. A debt to Watson
is acknowledged by every serious student and it still remains a
bible for everyone interested in Scottish history. Scotland's
place names give an extraordinary insight into its history
through which Watson acts as a guide. In authority and in
range it has never been superseded.

The book starts with a general survey before moving on to
deal with the Celtic names of each area. This is its first
paperback edition.

ISBN 1 874744 06 8
216 x 138mm, 576 pages
Paperback £14.99

THE SURNAMES OF SCOTLAND

George F. Black

Since it was first published in 1946, Black's *The Surnames of Scotland* has established itself as one of the great classics of genealogy. Listing over 8000 Scottish families alphabetically with a concise history of each, it is an essential tool for any genealogist, historian, or simply anyone with a general interest in Scotland. Despite its great length it is both clear and accessible.

Already in its tenth hardback printing, this is its first paperback and first UK edition.

ISBN 1 874744 07 6
216 x 138mm, 912 pages
Paperback £16.99